"I don't even know your name...but I feel as if we have some sort of connection."

Without warning, Grant bent and touched his lips to hers. Nina might have avoided the kiss, or pushed him away. But all she could do was stand there as waves of emotion crashed over her.

She took a step back and gazed at Grant. In the moonlight she saw his face—the dark, brooding eyes, the strong angle of his jaw, the way he was looking at her...

"Please don't," she whispered.

"Don't what?" His dark gaze enthralled her. "Don't touch you? Don't kiss you? Don't pursue you?"

All of those, she wanted to say.

In the crib beside them the baby fretted. Rather than breaking the tension, his soft sounds added to the turmoil inside Nina. Grant laughed softly and picked him up.

It was easy to see that Grant was a doting uncle. Nina wanted to take comfort in that fact. But how could she, when she had no way of knowing what he would do when he found out who she really was?

Dear Reader,

We're thrilled to bring you an *all-new*
LOST & FOUND!

Three women go into labor in the same Texas hospital,
and shortly after the babies are born, fire erupts.
Though each mother and baby make it to safety,
there's more than the mystery of birth to solve now....

Three of your favorite Intrigue writers have joined
together to bring you this special, *brand-new*
LOST & FOUND trilogy. Be sure to follow the story
over the next two months in *A Father for Her Baby* by
B.J. Daniels and *A Father's Love* by Carla Cassidy.

Happy reading!

Debra Matteucci
Senior Editor & Editorial Coordinator
Harlequin Books
300 East 42nd Street
New York, NY 10017

Somebody's Baby
Amanda Stevens

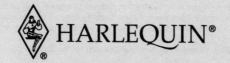

HARLEQUIN®

TORONTO • NEW YORK • LONDON
AMSTERDAM • PARIS • SYDNEY • HAMBURG
STOCKHOLM • ATHENS • TOKYO • MILAN • MADRID
PRAGUE • WARSAW • BUDAPEST • AUCKLAND

ISBN 0-373-22489-3

SOMEBODY'S BABY

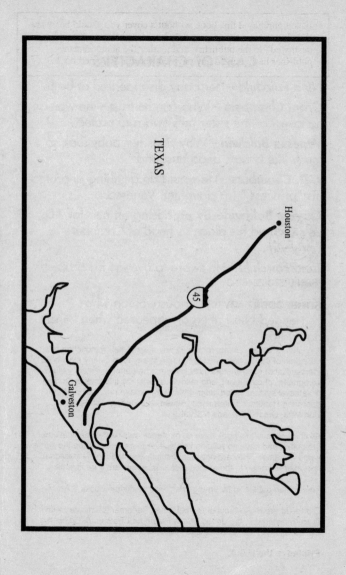

CAST OF CHARACTERS

Nina Fairchild—Her baby disappeared at birth.

Grant Chambers—Who can he trust—the woman he loves, or the sister he's sworn to protect?

Vanessa Baldwin—Why does her baby look so much like Nina's dead husband?

J. D. Chambers—He would do anything to protect his "princess," his daughter, Vanessa.

Clayton Baldwin—By producing an heir for J.D., he's secured his place as head of Chambers Petroleum.

Trent Fairchild—He swore to avenge his brother's death.

Karen Smith—A mysterious woman who befriended Nina, then disappeared when Nina's baby did.

Prologue

Nina Fairchild cradled her newborn son in her arms as she gazed down at him. He was so tiny and so perfect. So incredibly beautiful. Already she felt an extraordinary bond with this baby. He was the only family she had left.

If only you could be here to see our son, Garrett. If only you could hold Dustin in your arms.

Would it have made a difference? she wondered. Would this precious child have been able to save their marriage?

Nina had been haunted by that question ever since Garrett had died two weeks before she'd learned she was pregnant.

Pain twisted inside her as she stared down at her son. Because of her, Dustin would never know his father. Would he grow up to resent her for that? Would he hate her when he learned how his father had lost his life?

It's all your fault, Nina. Her brother-in-law's furious words rang in her ears. *Garrett is dead because of you, and somehow, some way, you're going to pay. I'll see to that.*

Nina shivered, remembering the darkness in Trent Fairchild's eyes. The warning in his voice.

The nurse leaned over Nina's bed to take the baby from her. Nina's arms tightened protectively around him. "Do you have to take him back so soon? I hate to let him out of my sight."

"You won't feel that way once you've gotten a few of those 2:00 a.m. feedings under your belt." The nurse lifted Dustin into her arms and smiled down at him. "He *is* a little beauty, isn't he? Look at that dark hair, and you so fair. But your sister has dark hair, doesn't she?"

Nina frowned. "My sister?"

"She was here earlier while you were in labor. She seemed real anxious about the delivery."

A tingle of alarm stole down Nina's backbone. "I don't have a sister."

The nurse, settling the baby in the cart to wheel him back to the nursery, glanced up, a cloud flitting across her features. "Then I must be wrong. I thought she said she was your sister, but we have two other mothers in labor and delivery tonight. The place is a madhouse, what with Dr. Bernard being detained and all."

"What did this woman look like?" Nina asked.

The nurse shrugged. "Late twenties. Petite. Dark hair. She wore glasses, I think."

Instantly an image of Karen Smith, a young woman who had befriended Nina in a Houston park several months ago, leaped to mind. But Karen had recently reconciled with her husband and moved away. What would she be doing here?

Nina hadn't told anyone she planned to have her baby at a small branch hospital in Galveston rather than at the huge medical complex in Houston. There was no way Karen could have found her. No way Trent Fairchild could have tracked her down here, either.

The nurse had to be mistaken, but the prickle of uneasiness wouldn't go away. Why would someone pretend to be Nina's sister? She didn't have a sister. Except for Dustin, she had no one.

"Is the woman still here?" she asked anxiously.

"I can check, but I don't think so. Visiting hours ended a long time ago. Speaking of which…" The nurse arched a stern brow. "It's time for this little guy to get his rest, and so should you." As if she sensed Nina's distress, her features softened. "Look, I wouldn't worry about it if I were you. I must have gotten the name wrong, that's all. Wouldn't be the first time, and like I said, it's been crazy around here all night."

The nurse's soothing tone helped calm Nina's fears. She was right, of course. It had to be a mistake. The months of worrying about Trent's threats had made her paranoid.

Nina got out of bed and leaned over the cart. Her long straight hair curtained her face, and she tucked it behind her ears as she stared down at her son. "I'll see you in a little while," she whispered.

"It'll come sooner than you think," the nurse told her. "So you'd better crawl back into that bed and get some sleep."

Nina smothered a yawn. "I *am* a little tired."

"Well, they don't call it labor for nothing, you know." She patted Nina's hand. "Now don't you worry. I'll bring him back in a few hours for his feeding."

"I can hardly wait," Nina murmured as she bent to kiss her baby's satiny cheek one last time.

NINA AWAKENED sometime later, her heart pounding in fear. At first she thought the wails and screams she heard were echoes from the nightmare she'd been having about the car crash that had taken Garrett's life. But then, coming more fully awake, she realized the cacophony of terror was all too real. Panicked voices sounded from the hallway outside her door, and from the street three stories below her window, the scream of sirens rose to an almost unbearable crescendo.

An acrid scent stung her mouth and throat, and Nina's panic mushroomed as she recognized the smell. Smoke!

Was the hospital on fire?

Dear God, Dustin! She had to get to her baby…make sure he was okay…get him to safety….

Her frantic thoughts spiraling out of control, Nina struggled out of bed and slipped on her robe as she crossed the room slowly, her muscles still weak from her labor. As she opened the door, the pandemonium of a full-scale evacuation erupted down the corridor.

Nina started down the hallway, trailing the exodus. She grabbed a passing nurse's arm, and the woman whirled, her face a tightly controlled mask of fear. "Where did you come from?" she demanded.

Nina pointed down the hallway. "Room 317. What's happening?"

"This floor is being evacuated. There's a fire."

Nina's hand tightened on the woman's arm. "The nursery is on this floor!"

The woman hesitated, then said, "Don't worry.

The babies would have been the first to be moved. You should have already been out of here, too.''

"No one came to my room,'' Nina said. "I was asleep.''

The nurse's eyes widened in alarm, but she shrugged helplessly and shook off Nina's hand. "Just go. Head for the stairs. Do you need assistance?''

"No, I'm all right.'' But when the woman turned away, Nina sagged against the wall, her strength waning. The sprinklers had come on, and she was soaked. Her robe felt like an iron mantle around her shoulders as she pushed herself away from the wall and staggered down the hallway. But rather than heading for the emergency exit, she turned the other way, toward the nursery.

Don't worry. The babies would have been the first to be moved.

But Nina had seen the doubt in the woman's eyes. She couldn't be sure the babies had been evacuated, and neither could Nina. No one had come for *her,* had they? How could she be certain Dustin had been removed from harm's way unless she checked for herself?

The corridors were eerily deserted now, but Nina could still hear shouts in the distance. As she rounded a corner, a man in green scrubs hurried by her. Nina recognized him. He was the young resident who had delivered Dustin.

"Dr. Wharton!''

The man stopped and glanced over his shoulder. When he saw Nina, he slipped something into the pocket of his scrubs, but he made no move to join her. His face showed more impatience than fear, and not one shred of recognition. "Who are you?" he asked. "What the hell are you still doing in here?"

Nina put out a hand in supplication. "Please help me. You delivered my baby earlier. A little boy. I have to make sure he's okay."

"The nursery's already been evacuated. I just came from there."

Nina took a shaky step toward him. "Are you sure?"

He fingered the pocket of his scrubs. "Yeah. Everyone's split. Now I suggest we do the same."

Not waiting for a response, he turned and strode away, leaving Nina wavering in the hallway. Dustin was safe, she told herself. He had to be. But something inside her wouldn't allow her to leave without making sure. If she hadn't left Garrett that night, he might still be alive. He might have been here to witness the birth of his son.

Holding her robe against her nose and mouth, Nina located the nursery and gazed through the glass partition. The babies were gone, thank God. Now she had to get herself to safety.

But the smoke had suddenly grown so thick, she became disoriented. Terror washed over her. She looked up and saw flames eating through the ceiling tiles.

She hurried down the hallway. Just as she saw the glow of the exit sign ahead, a new premonition of danger stole over her. Glancing back, she caught a movement out of the corner of her eye. Someone was still in the building with her.

She started to call out, but suddenly a portion of the ceiling collapsed and something hit her head.

Pain shot through her skull as she fell, stunned and terrified, to the floor.

Coughing, struggling for breath, Nina turned her last conscious thought to Dustin. If she didn't make it out of here alive, who would take care of her son?

NINA CAME TO ABRUPTLY, fear exploding inside her. She was trapped inside a burning building! She had to get out! She had to find Dustin!

But when she tried to rise, she was pushed back down. Something covered her mouth and nose, and in a full-blown panic, she fought to remove it. Again a strong hand stilled her action.

"Take it easy," a man's voice said. "You're going to be fine. We're giving you oxygen. You inhaled quite a bit of smoke, but I don't think there's any serious damage to your lungs. We'll know for sure when we get you to a hospital."

Nina's mind whirled in confusion. She lay quiet for a moment, trying to orient herself. Trying to make sense of what had happened. The hospital had somehow caught fire and was apparently still burning. The blaze reddened the sky above her, and she could still hear the shouts of the firemen and the sound of the pumps gushing water. She'd been trapped inside the hospital, knocked unconscious, but now she was outside, lying on the ground while someone—a doctor, she presumed—hovered over her.

He allowed her to lift the oxygen mask long enough to croak, "What happened? How did I get out here?"

"One of the firemen found you inside. You were lucky they double-checked the building. We thought we had everyone out. What were you doing in there anyway? Never mind,'' he said quickly when she started to remove the mask again. ''Don't try to talk. Just lie still. As soon as an ambulance is available, we'll get you to another hospital.''

Nina motioned frantically at the mask, and with a sigh of impatience, he lifted it once again. She swallowed, trying to ease the burning pain in her throat. ''Where did they take my baby?'' she asked hoarsely.

''Your baby was in the nursery?'' When Nina nodded, he said, ''All the newborns were taken to St. Mary's in Houston. They have an excellent neonatal ICU, but don't worry. It's just a precaution. My understanding is that all of the infants are fine.''

Her worst fears calmed for the moment, Nina tried to relax, but it was upsetting to think of Dustin, so tiny and vulnerable, all alone in Houston, while she lay on the ground outside a burning hospital in Galveston. He was only a few hours old and already they'd been separated.

How could this have happened? Nina wondered. How could a hospital catch fire and burn so quickly?

''I'll have you transferred to St. Mary's so you can be with your baby.'' The doctor jotted something on a notepad. He lifted her hand to glance at her wrist, then frowned. ''Your hospital ID bracelet is missing. Any idea what happened to it?''

Nina shook her head. Right now a missing ID bracelet was the least of her worries.

The doctor, however, seemed overly concerned about it. His scowl deepened. ''You usually have to cut those things off. They don't just fall off by themselves.''

Was it her imagination, or was there a hint of suspicion in the man's words and in the way he glanced down at her?

"I'll need your name," he said, lifting the oxygen mask from her mouth. "And your room number. Later there may be other questions."

BY THE TIME NINA WAS finally transported to the emergency room at St. Mary's, she'd been taken off the oxygen. Her breathing was even, but still painful. She was exhausted, her throat and chest ached and the horrors of the past few hours still haunted her. But all she wanted was to see her baby.

When a doctor finally came into the cubicle to examine her, Nina pleaded with him to let her see her son. "Please. He's all I've got."

Dropping his air of professionalism for a moment, the doctor nodded sympathetically. He turned to the nurse behind him. "Go see what you can find out about the Fairchild baby. Let me know as soon as you hear something."

When the nurse exited the room, Nina said, "Thank you. I have to know he's all right. I've been so worried—"

"No need to thank me." His tone was brisk. "I have kids of my own. Now, try to get some rest. We'll send you upstairs as soon as a bed becomes available. Then you'll be able to see your son for yourself."

Just as he was about to leave, the nurse hurried back into the cubicle. She murmured something in the doctor's ear, and with a quick glance at Nina, the two dashed out.

Nina tried to tell herself whatever was wrong had

nothing to do with Dustin. The emergency room was chaotic. The doctor was probably needed elsewhere, some life-or-death crisis that would explain the tense look on his face.

But when he came back into the cubicle a few moments later, a new terror seized her. Something was definitely wrong.

"What's the matter with my baby?" She hardly recognized her own voice. It sounded far too calm, far too in control to belong to someone who was paralyzed with such fear. "What's wrong with Dustin? I want to see him."

"I'm afraid that's impossible at the moment."

"Oh, my God." Nina's chest tightened. Dizziness swept over her, and for a moment, she wanted to succumb to the darkness. Wanted to hide from what she was about to learn. "My baby…is he…?"

The doctor took her hand. "I'm sure your baby is fine. No cause for alarm, but…it seems there's been some sort of mix-up. Your baby isn't here."

Nina stared at him in confusion, uncertain whether to feel relief or despair. What did he mean, Dustin wasn't here? If he wasn't here, where was he? "I don't understand. I was told my son was brought to this hospital. Where is he? Why can't I see him? What's happened to him?"

"We're making some calls right now. Some of the patients from Galveston were taken to other area hospitals. We'll find your baby, Mrs. Fairchild. There's no reason to worry."

No reason to worry? Her baby was missing, and this man was advising her not to worry?

After he'd left the cubicle again, Nina lay there and tried to think what to do. What *could* she do?

She wasn't in any condition to get up and start a search herself, and yet the thought of entrusting her baby's safety to complete strangers was almost overwhelming. Did they have any idea what Dustin meant to her? How much she loved him? How much she *needed* him?

He had to be all right, Nina told herself, but as much as she wanted to believe in the power of positive thinking, she knew firsthand how wrong things could go. Hadn't she prayed for Garrett's safety on the roadside that night? Hadn't she told herself he would be all right if she left him long enough to go for help?

Inadvertently an image of Trent Fairchild materialized in her mind. She could see his handsome face contorted with rage, the cold, black hatred in his eyes as he'd glared down at her at the funeral. *It's all your fault, Nina. Garrett is dead because of you, and somehow, some way, you're going to pay. I'll see to that.*

Dear God, was this her punishment? Was Dustin being taken from her because of what she'd done to Garrett?

When the door to the cubicle opened again, Nina jumped. The doctor walked slowly to her bedside, his expression grim. Nina's heart began to pound. She tried to look away from him, but couldn't. As adept as she was at protecting her emotions, concealing her fears, there was no hiding from this. No running away from the truth.

"I'm going to be straight with you, Mrs. Fairchild." The gentleness of his tone almost did her in. She clutched the bed sheets in her fists as her throat knotted with fear.

"So far, we haven't been able to locate your son. I still believe there's been some sort of mix-up with Galveston, and in a few hours we'll get it all sorted out. You'll be holding your son in your arms in no time. But meanwhile..." His voice trailed off as his gaze dropped from hers. "Just to be on the safe side, we're calling in the police...."

Chapter One

Six months later

"Sergeant Farrell, please." Nina fastened her long hair into a ponytail as she waited on hold. She knew from experience it could take several minutes for Boyd Farrell to answer his phone, so she used the time to scan the web page she'd designed for a local bookstore.

Nina loved her job. Designing web pages for small businesses who wanted to join the information superhighway was uniquely exciting. But working at home also had its drawbacks. Always somewhat of a loner, Nina would sometimes go for days without seeing another soul, and she knew that wasn't particularly healthy. Perhaps that was why she'd been so susceptible to Karen Smith's overtures of friendship. Perhaps that's why she hadn't recognized the woman's deception.

"Sergeant Farrell," a masculine voice said in her ear.

"It's Nina."

She could imagine him running a hand through his thinning, light brown hair, perhaps staring at the framed picture of his wife and daughter on his desk while he figured out a tactful way to get rid of her.

"How are you, Nina?"

"Hanging in there." She forced an optimism into her tone. "What's the latest?"

She heard him sigh and tried to steel herself against the inevitable disappointment. "There's nothing new on the case. You know I would have called you if there were."

Of course she knew that, but she still couldn't help hoping. Every time she called him, she couldn't help hoping.

"No leads on Karen Smith?"

Another pause. The questions were always the same. So were the answers. "Afraid not."

"She couldn't have just vanished from the face of the earth," Nina insisted. "She's out there somewhere with my baby."

"We don't know for sure who took your baby. We have to keep an open mind, Nina. Dustin's kidnapping could have been random. Any one of the infants in that nursery could have been taken during the fire."

"But they weren't," she countered. "Only Dustin. If he wasn't singled out, why was my ID bracelet missing? Was that just some strange coincidence?"

"I don't know," Farrell admitted.

She pressed her point. "You know as well as I do the evidence points to Karen Smith—the way she met me in the park that day, how she kept coming back until we became friends and she found out everything about me. If she didn't take Dustin, why did she just disappear like that? Why haven't you been able to find a Karen Smith who fits her description?"

They'd covered this ground so many times, but to Farrell's credit, he always responded with patience. "Like I've told you before, it's possible the woman was a professional. She could have scoped you out ahead of time, found out you were alone and pregnant and decided you'd be an easy target. At this point, we just don't know. But, Nina, if a professional did take your baby—"

"I know." She closed her eyes, not wanting to think about the possibilities, even after all this time. If Karen Smith had taken Dustin, it probably wasn't to keep him, but to broker him—to sell him to someone desperate for a baby. Even if they found Karen, there were no guarantees she would lead them to Dustin.

"What about the fire?" Nina finally asked. "Any leads there?"

"The arson investigators haven't closed the case, but there's still nothing conclusive."

"You and I both know she set the fire. She was there that night, pretending to be my sister."

"Unfortunately we don't have any corroborating evidence on that, either," Farrell reminded her. "The nurse you spoke with that night thinks she may have been mistaken about the person claiming to be your sister. And no one else remembers seeing a dark-haired woman hanging around Labor and Delivery."

"But she *was* there," Nina said bitterly. "She burned an entire hospital to the ground so that she could take my son and disappear with him. Why haven't you been able to find her? Why haven't you done something, *anything* to put that woman behind bars and bring my son back to me?"

Six months of grief and frustration trembled in

Nina's voice, and it was all she could do to suppress her emotions. But breaking down wouldn't help find Dustin. She had to remain calm, in control. She had to keep Sergeant Farrell on her side.

"I'm sorry," she murmured. "That wasn't fair."

"I've been wondering when it would happen. Your restraint has been nothing short of remarkable." Something crept into his voice that Nina couldn't quite define. "Believe me, I'm doing everything I can to find Dustin."

She wanted to be encouraged by his words, but six months was a long time. An eternity. Even a mother's hope couldn't stay alive forever. She fought back the sting of tears. "I know you are. Please, Sergeant. Just don't give up."

"I won't," he promised. "And you hang in there. I'll talk to you next week, okay?"

Nina took a deep breath, mustering her fragile resolve. "Okay."

As always, when she severed the call, it seemed as if she'd cut away a piece of her heart. No news, no witnesses, no leads of any kind. After all this time, the trail had grown so cold, she knew it would take a miracle to find her baby.

And as Nina knew from experience, miracles were very hard to come by.

Chapter Two

"Grant, I swear," Vanessa Baldwin drawled. "I've never seen a man take to a baby the way you have to John David. You've been back from Caracas, what, three weeks? And already you've spoiled that child rotten." She toyed nervously with a pink diamond that lay in the hollow of her throat.

Grant's sister was as beautiful as always, but she looked a little more fragile than he remembered. He wondered if she was taking care of herself, if she was taking her medication as she was supposed to.

He arched a brow in her direction. "So what if I *am* spoiling the little guy. Isn't that what an uncle's supposed to do?"

They were sitting in Grant's office at Chambers Petroleum while Vanessa waited for her husband, Clayton Baldwin, the company's vice president, to finish with his meeting. A meeting that had ominously excluded Grant.

Since returning from a four-year stint in the Venezuelan oil fields, Grant had found it harder than he'd expected to assimilate himself back into the political machinations of the company. His return had renewed speculation regarding his father's successor at Chambers Petroleum. As J. D. Chambers's only son, Grant should have been the leading contender for that position. But four years ago, he'd managed to land himself in the middle of a scandal that had proved almost ruinous to the company and to the family. His subsequent exile to the Venezuelan jungle had been his retribution and, considering the success of the venture, his redemption.

But in Grant's absence, his strongest competitor, Clayton Baldwin, had managed to get himself promoted to vice president, marry the boss's daughter and—the coup de grâce—present J. D. Chambers with his only grandchild. A son, no less. The only Chambers heir.

Grant stared down at the baby he held on his lap and tried to muster a little resentment. But it was no use. When he looked at his nephew, all he saw was a cute kid with a toothless grin. A nearly bald little charmer who had managed to wrap his uncle around his little finger.

Visions of baseball games and hot-dog stands danced in Grant's head.

"…just can't wait around forever," Vanessa was saying. "You don't have any idea how long Clayton and Daddy will be in that meeting with the Ventura people?"

"I wasn't made privy to their agenda," Grant said dryly.

His sister frowned. "Oh, Grant. You know I despise this competition between you and Clayton. It just doesn't seem fair. Why should I be put in the position of having to choose between my brother and my husband?"

"It's not exactly your choice," Grant reminded her.

"I know, but I can't help wishing—" Vanessa broke off, biting her lip.

"That I would bow out gracefully?"

Her blue eyes took on a repentant look. "I know how much you love this company. You've worked like a dog since high school. But, Grant, I honestly can't see you settling down to run Chambers Petroleum. The day-to-day details would bore you to tears."

He glanced at her. "And not Clayton?"

"He's a family man now. He has responsibilities. He's matured a lot since you've been gone."

And grown into an even bigger jerk, Grant thought but refrained from saying so. He made a face at the baby instead, and John David laughed, waving his arms appreciatively. Grant settled him at his shoulder, so the little boy could look out the window behind them.

Vanessa's expression grew puzzled. "How do you do that?"

"What?"

"Act so…I don't know…natural with him. You've never been around babies. I didn't even think you liked kids."

Grant shrugged. "Neither did I, but John David and I just hit it off. Didn't we, buddy?"

As if in agreement, the baby gurgled and laughed, then promptly spit up on Grant's shoulder.

Vanessa jumped to her feet. "Oh, no. Grant, you'll positively reek for the rest of the day."

"I've smelled worse, believe me. You haven't lived until you've been in the jungle for two months at a stretch.'' Calmly, Grant handed John David to Vanessa, then reached for the baby wipes she put on his desk. Vanessa held the child gingerly, as if afraid he would spit up on her pink suit.

Grant didn't understand why his sister seemed so uneasy with the baby. John David was six months old. Surely Vanessa should be used to motherhood by now, but in the three weeks Grant had been home, he had begun to notice a disturbing pattern. Both Vanessa and Clayton talked incessantly about the baby, but neither of them seemed to spend much time with him. John David was usually in the care of his nanny.

And as if on cue, Alice Becker came bustling into Grant's office. She looked windblown and frazzled, but rather than letting her catch her breath, Vanessa stood and handed her the baby. ''You're late.''

''I'm so sorry, Mrs. Baldwin,'' the woman said contritely. ''It won't happen again.''

''I hope not.'' Vanessa turned to Grant. ''I can't wait any longer for Clayton. Will you tell him I stopped by?''

''Sure.''

To the nanny, she said, ''I have another appointment near here, but I'll take you and the baby home first.''

''Oh, I was hoping you could drop us at the park,'' Alice said, her eyes lowered. ''We could both do with some fresh air.''

Vanessa frowned. ''I'm sure you could, but thanks to my husband, I'm running late enough as it is. The park is out of the question. By the time I take you all the way home—''

"What are you talking about?" Grant interjected. "There's a park right across the street."

"What?" Vanessa whirled, her blue eyes wide with surprise, as if she had somehow forgotten his presence.

Grant pointed to the window. "Mirror Lake Park is just across the street. It'd be a shame for John David to be cooped up in the house on such a beautiful day. Why don't you drop him and Mrs. Becker off at the park, then pick them up when you finish with your appointment? It would even save you from having to take them all the way home first."

Vanessa's lips tightened almost imperceptibly. "My appointment could take a couple of hours."

"Oh, I wouldn't mind," the nanny chirped in. "Mr. Chambers is right. The weather is beautiful." She threw him a dazzling smile, which Grant briefly acknowledged, then glanced away. He didn't want to give her encouragement. In the few times he'd been in Alice Becker's presence, she'd made him decidedly uncomfortable.

"There was a mugging in Mirror Lake Park a few weeks ago," Vanessa said. "I don't think it's safe."

Grant laughed. "You're just being an overprotective mother. Every park in Houston has the occasional mugging. Mirror Lake is perfectly safe, especially in the middle of the day."

Vanessa bit her lip. "I don't know." She glanced at Alice Becker and John David, obviously torn by what seemed to Grant an inconsequential decision. Then she shrugged. "I suppose it'll be okay. But look—" she tapped her diamond watch with her fingertip "—I want you to have the baby in the parking lot at a quarter of one. I don't want to have to go tramping all over the park looking for you."

"Of course, Mrs. Baldwin." Alice Becker sent Grant another smile, then bent to retrieve John David's diaper bag. Slinging it over her shoulder, she competently shifted the baby to her other hip and hurried out of the office.

Vanessa gave Grant a sour look. "See what you've done. As if that woman wasn't smitten enough before—"

"Don't even start," Grant warned. He came around the desk to give his sister a peck on the cheek. "And stop worrying. It's just an afternoon in the park. They'll be fine."

"Easy for you to say," Vanessa fretted. "You don't know what it's like to be a parent."

"No, I guess I don't."

If there was regret in his tone, Vanessa seemed not to notice. She picked up her purse and headed for the door. "Don't forget about tonight," she called. "The party is in your honor, so don't even think about not showing up."

"That was the old Grant. You're looking at the new and improved version."

She paused at the door and glanced back. "Not too new and improved, I hope. I sort of liked you as the black sheep."

"Only because it made you look so good."

Vanessa smiled, her pink-tinted lips curling in amusement. But there was something in her eyes, a glimmer of emotion Grant couldn't quite define. "You always did know me too well," she murmured.

THE PARK WAS nearly deserted. It seemed lonelier than usual without the shouts and laughter of the children, but most of them were still in school this time of day.

Perhaps it was just as well, Nina thought, walking along a leaf-strewn pathway. Though she'd haunted the park—the last place she'd seen Karen Smith— for months, the children were always a painful reminder of her loss.

Lifting her face to the sky, Nina drew a long breath. The sun warmed her face and shoulders, but the coldness inside her lingered. Six months, she thought numbly. Six long months without a trace.

Where was Dustin at this moment? Was he happy? Was he being taken care of? Or was he...?

Nina closed her eyes briefly. Most of the time, she was able to keep the terror at bay, but there were times like today when every mother's nightmare tormented her. Her baby was missing, and she had no idea where he was or who had him. Had he been hurt? Was he still alive?

Abruptly Nina turned down another path, heading toward the deserted playground. Finding a bench, she sat down, her thoughts spiraling back to the days when she'd come to the park after Garrett's death, when a tiny life growing inside her had been all that had kept her from despair.

Nina scanned her surroundings. *What are you looking for? Did you think Karen Smith would simply appear out of the blue and give you back your son? Is that why you came here today? Is that why you always come here?*

It had been a day very much like today when she'd first met Karen in the park. The sun had been shining then, too, but the weather had been cooler. Nina had worn a loose sweater over jeans, and although her pregnancy had not yet been outwardly noticeable, she'd been fascinated by all the changes occurring within her body. She'd been sitting alone on a bench that day, hand on her stomach, when she'd felt her baby move for the first time.

Startled at first, she sat stone still, unsure what was happening to her. Then the tiny flutter came again, and Nina laughed out loud, marveling at the miracle growing inside her.

"Excuse me."

Nina glanced up to find a dark-haired woman standing over her. She was petite and very pretty, her blue eyes softly glowing behind black-rimmed glasses. She smiled knowingly, as if she shared Nina's secret.

"You're pregnant, aren't you?"

Nina stared at her in surprise. "How did you know?"

The woman's smile turned shy. "I've been watching you. I've seen you here before. You always keep one hand on your stomach. See?"

She nodded, and Nina glanced down. Her hand was still resting against her stomach. Almost self-consciously she removed it.

The woman sat down beside her. "I only noticed because I did the same thing when I was pregnant. It was the most wonderful experience in the world." She broke off and glanced down. "I'm sorry. You must think I'm crazy, coming over here like this."

"No," Nina said impulsively. "No, I don't. I know exactly what you mean. It *is* wonderful. So wonderful you want to share it with someone."

And Nina had no one. It hadn't hit her until that moment how truly alone she was. No friends, no family, no one with whom to share this blessing.

And Karen Smith seemed just as lonely. There was something about her that immediately drew Nina to her. Perhaps it was the shadow of pain in the woman's eyes or the self-conscious way she had of dipping her head, as if she didn't quite have the courage to look you in the eye. Perhaps it was because Karen had suffered a great loss, too, miscarrying three months into her pregnancy.

Nina could relate to all of those things. She and Karen were like kindred spirits. They began meeting in the park almost daily, their conversations revolving around Nina's baby at first. But then gradually, as their friendship deepened and Nina's pregnancy progressed, she found herself confiding in Karen as she had never been able to do with anyone else. Not even with her husband.

She told Karen about her impulsive marriage to Garrett, how he had swept her off her feet and how his family had despised her from the first, how they thought she was nothing but a gold digger after the Fairchild money. She told Karen about her insecurities and how she had allowed Garrett's family to use them against her. How in the end, he had chosen his family over her.

Karen had been so sympathetic, the perfect listener. How could Nina have known it was all just pretend, that the deception had begun the moment Karen had approached her in the park that day?

"Excuse me."

Nina was so caught up in her reverie, that when a woman's voice spoke in front of her, she jumped.

She looked up, almost expecting—hoping—to see Karen Smith, but the woman who gazed down at her was a stranger. Her plump, round face had none of Karen's fragile beauty, and her hair—rather than dark and exotic—was a light mousy brown.

The woman, pushing a baby carriage, indicated the bench beside Nina. "Would you mind if we sit here? He's a little fussy. I think he's ready for his bottle."

Nina swallowed and nodded. She hadn't been this close to a baby since the day Dustin was born. Her arms ached when the woman lifted the child from the stroller and settled him on her lap.

Nina tried not to look. She tried to glance away, but the baby's obvious distress drew her attention in spite of herself.

She couldn't tell much about his features, other than the fact that he had almost no hair. His face was red and puckered, and for a long moment, no sound came out of his mouth. Then he finally caught his breath, stiffened his body, threw back his head and let loose a wail that could have been heard two city blocks away.

Nina watched in fascination as the woman struggled to quiet him. She reached forward, fishing in an overflowing diaper bag for a bottle as the child screamed and squirmed on her lap.

She gave Nina an apologetic glance. "He's teething, too."

"Can I help?" Nina asked hesitantly.

"I can't find his bottle," the woman said in exasperation. "I know I packed it."

"Maybe you left it in the car," Nina suggested.

The woman cut her a look. "I hope not. His mother dropped us off. We don't usually come to this park. There's one much closer to the house, but Mrs. Baldwin had an appointment and this one was more convenient. She won't be back for a while.'' The woman held the child with one arm while rummaging through the diaper bag. ''John David, be still. You're only making things worse.''

After a few more moments, the woman gave up. ''Maybe you *can* help.''

Nina reached for the diaper bag, but the woman raised the baby in her arms instead. ''Do you mind?''

Nina hesitated. *Don't do this,* a little voice warned. *Don't torture yourself. Don't remind yourself of what might have been.*

But it was no use. She could no more have stopped herself from taking that baby than she could have prevented the sun from coming up in the morning.

A nun in the orphanage where Nina had been raised once told her that she was born to be a mother. That someday all the love she had stored up inside her would be lavished on her own children. And they would adore her in return. Nina had dreamed of that day. Lived for the moment when she would finally hold her baby—her own flesh and blood—in her arms.

Her throat tightened as she held the writhing child against her, drinking in the sweetness of him. The innocence.

He looked to be about six months old, as Dustin would be now, and what little hair he had was dark, as Dustin's had been. The child stirred something powerful in Nina she didn't understand. He was a stranger, and yet so many emotions rushed over her. What was happening to her?

''It's okay, sweetie,'' she crooned, cradling him

against her as she rocked to and fro. "Everything's okay."

"His bottle isn't in here," the woman beside her muttered. "I don't know what could have happened to it. Mrs. Baldwin must have taken it out, though for the life of me—" She turned with a teething ring and handed it to Nina. "Here, let's try this."

Nina did as she was told, but the baby promptly shoved the useless plastic away. "You're hungry, aren't you?" she murmured.

The woman sighed. "I'm afraid he'll just have to wait until his mother gets here."

She reached for the baby, but Nina said quickly, "Oh, may I please hold him for a little longer? I think he's starting to quiet."

The woman looked doubtful. "I've imposed on you long enough."

"It's no imposition. Please. Just a minute more." There was a desperate note in Nina's voice she didn't recognize. Why was it so important she hold on to this child? He was a stranger and she was acting as if—

"You've been very kind." The woman's tone grew insistent. "But I'll take the baby now."

"Please—"

"Give me the child!"

The fear in the woman's eyes startled Nina. What on earth was she doing? She'd frightened the poor woman half to death, and all because she'd wanted to hold the baby in her arms a little longer. Wanted to pretend a little longer.

"I—I'm sorry," she stammered. Just as she was about to hand the child back, she saw a man striding toward them. He was tall and broad shouldered with thick black hair and—Nina saw when he drew closer—gray eyes that were very dark and very piercing.

The woman beside her looked enormously relieved when she spotted him. She jumped up from the bench and grabbed his arm. "Mr. Chambers! I'm so glad to see you!"

His dark gaze went from the woman to Nina, and then to the baby she still held on her lap. His eyes narrowed. "What's going on?" he demanded, in a voice every bit as dark and deep as his eyes.

As if also affected by the man's sudden appearance, the baby on Nina's lap grew still, staring up at the stranger with rapt attention.

"She won't give the baby back to me!" the woman said in a shrill voice. "She insisted on holding him while I looked for his bottle, and then she wouldn't give him back to me."

Nina winced. "No, please, it wasn't like that. I can explain—"

The man walked over and took the baby from her with such authority, Nina shrank away from him. He swung the child up into his arms, and John David laughed delightedly, momentarily forgetting his hunger pains.

With the flair of a magician, the man produced a bottle from his jacket pocket. "I thought you might be needing this," he said to the woman beside him. "Vanessa left it in my office."

"Oh, thank heavens," she exclaimed, taking both baby and bottle from the man. "You're a lifesaver, Mr. Chambers." She settled the baby in the stroller and gave him his bottle. The baby instantly quieted.

The woman straightened and glared at Nina. "Should we call the police?"

The man nodded toward the parking lot. "Why don't you take John David back to my car? Vanessa should be here soon."

"Yes, sir." With one last look at Nina, the woman turned and headed across the park.

Nina tore her gaze from the departing stroller and glanced up at the stranger. He towered over her, looking dark and grim and more formidable that she would have ever thought possible.

He was very handsome in a tough and arrogant sort of way. The casualness of his apparel—jeans, boots and a lightweight leather jacket—didn't fool her. He had the look and demeanor of a man who had power and money and knew how to use both to his advantage.

He reminded her of the Fairchilds, and Nina felt a sudden stab of resentment. Who was he to judge her? He didn't know her. He didn't know anything about her.

"I wasn't going to hurt your baby," she said. "I would never do that. I...just wanted to hold him."

He said sharply, "Who are you?"

"I'm no one. I didn't mean any harm. I'll go quietly away, and you'll never see me again."

He caught her arm when she stood. A thrill of fear shot through her as his gaze probed her face. "Why do I get the feeling I know you from somewhere?"

"You don't." Nina forced her tone to remain even. "I've never seen you before. I wanted to hold your baby because I—" She started to explain about Dustin, then broke off. "It doesn't matter why. I'm sorry."

Was it her imagination or had his features softened? He was still gazing down at her with a quizzical look in his eyes. "No harm done, I guess." His hand fell away from her arm. "But I would be careful from now on if I were you. People are very protective when it comes to their children. Someone might get the wrong idea, and you could find yourself in some pretty serious trouble."

Without waiting for a response, he turned and strode away. Nina waited for a few minutes, then took a circuitous route to the parking lot, hoping he would be gone by the time she arrived at her car. But as she reached to unlock her door, she saw him.

He was standing beside a silver BMW, bending slightly to talk to the blond woman inside. The other woman—the nanny, Nina presumed—was busy fastening the baby into his car seat. Then she climbed into the back with him while the man stored the stroller in the trunk. He said another quick word to the blonde, then she started the engine and backed out of the parking slot.

Nina hurriedly climbed into her own car, hoping she wouldn't be detected. But as the silver BMW approached Nina's parking space, the blonde slowed the car, waiting for a truck that had backed out in front of her. Her window was still down, and as she drew even with Nina's car, she glanced over, then away, then back again. Their gazes locked.

It was one of those life-defining moments. One of those impossible coincidences. It couldn't really be happening, and yet there she was.

Nina's breath left her in a painful rush as she stared at the woman behind the wheel. The hair color was different, as was her expression and demeanor. But her eyes…something about her eyes…

For one split second, both women seemed frozen in time. Then the blonde whipped her head around, and the car shot forward. But the shock on her face mirrored Nina's. She'd recognized Nina, too, and for one very good reason.

The woman in the silver BMW was Karen Smith.

Chapter Three

"Sergeant Farrell, please." Nina tried to catch her breath while she waited for the detective to answer his phone. She still couldn't believe it had happened. How many times had she gone to that park since Dustin had disappeared, hoping to find him, hoping to see Karen Smith?

When the car first sped away, Nina had tried her best to follow, but once they'd left the park, traffic thickened on Memorial. The best she could do was keep the silver car in sight, but eventually even that proved fruitless. The BMW was much faster than Nina's compact. Without warning, it had shot up an on-ramp to the freeway and was soon lost in the steady stream of traffic heading toward downtown while Nina sat on the feeder lane, stuck behind two 18-wheelers.

Dustin had been so close. So close! She'd actually held him in her arms!

Nina swallowed a sob. Her baby was alive! He'd appeared healthy and unharmed, and...dear God, she'd held him in her arms.

"Sergeant Farrell."

Nina gulped air, trying to calm her racing heart. "It's Nina. You won't believe what just happened."

"Nina." His sigh was audible. "Haven't we already spoken today?"

"Yes, but something wonderful has happened. A miracle." She paused for another breath. "I saw Dustin. I saw my baby! I held him! All we have to do now is go get him. You'll help me, won't you? You have to—"

"Nina, slow down. What do you mean, you saw Dustin?"

"At Mirror Lake Park. I go there every day. A part of me has always hoped I'd find him, but today it happened. It really happened." Nina gripped the phone so tightly her knuckles hurt. Soon her baby would be back in her arms. Soon Dustin would be home where he belonged. She pictured the yellow-and-white nursery, awaiting his return.

"You saw him in Mirror Lake Park." Something in Farrell's tone pierced the cloud of excitement surrounding Nina. She gripped the phone even tighter.

"That's what I said. He was there with a woman, his nanny, I think, and she let me hold him. She called him John David. His last name is Baldwin, or Chambers, I'm not really sure which, but it doesn't matter, because his real name is Dustin Fairchild. You believe me, don't you?"

There was the briefest hesitation before Farrell said slowly, "You saw a woman in the park with a baby. What makes you think that baby was Dustin?"

"Because I also saw Karen Smith."

"You *what?*"

At last she seemed to have gotten his attention. Nina let out a relieved breath. She'd gone about this all wrong. She should have told him about Karen Smith first, but her baby had been uppermost in her mind. No wonder Sergeant Farrell couldn't make sense of her babbling.

"Let me start at the beginning," she said.

"I think that might be a good idea."

Nina quickly told him everything that had happened in the park, except the nanny's accusation that Nina had refused to give the baby back to her. Nina's actions had hardly been those of a rational woman, and she desperately needed Sergeant Farrell to believe her. More than anything, she needed him to believe her.

"I couldn't keep up with the car," she finished. "But I did manage to get the license-plate number." She rattled off the number, then said, "You can trace the vehicle, right?"

Again Farrell hesitated. "Nina, are you sure about all this?"

"Of course I'm sure. I couldn't be mistaken about something like this. My baby's life is at stake." Nina felt a wave of hysteria rising inside her, but with sheer force of will, pushed it back down.

"You said the woman in the BMW was blond. Karen Smith had dark hair. At least that's what you've always maintained."

"She could have dyed her hair or worn a wig. It makes sense she would have disguised herself. She was planning all along to steal my baby."

"That part does make sense," he conceded with a sigh. "But it's still a little hard to swallow that you saw Karen Smith in the same park where you first met her. If she took Dustin, why would she go back there, knowing she might eventually run into you?"

"The nanny said they didn't usually go to that park, but the baby's mother—she called her Mrs. Baldwin—had an appointment near there. That makes sense, too, when you think about it. After all this time, Karen probably thought she was home free. It was a one-in-a-million chance that I saw her at all today."

"You say her name is Baldwin?" Farrell seemed preoccupied, as if he were jotting notes to himself.

"Yes, and the man's name is Chambers, but I don't know what his relationship is to Dustin." Was he a conspirator in her baby's abduction? Nina shivered, remembering the man's eyes, the menacing way he'd stared down at her. "You do believe me, don't you? You are going to follow up on this, aren't you?"

"I'll check it out," Farrell agreed noncommittally. "As soon as we find out who the car belongs to, we can decide where to go from there."

"How long will that be?"

"I'll run it through the computer as soon as we hang up. But look. You said it yourself. It's a million-to-one shot that you and Karen Smith came face-to-face in that same park."

"Meaning?"

He paused. "Don't get your hopes up, okay?"

NINA WAS WAITING at her desk when Sergeant Farrell called back a little later. She grabbed up the phone on the first ring.

"Did you find her?"

"I ran the plate number," Farrell said. "The car is registered to a Mrs. Vanessa Baldwin. It's a Houston address. River Oaks," he added, naming Houston's most prestigious—and expensive—neighborhood.

A flood of memories washed over Nina. Garrett's family lived in a San Antonio neighborhood very much like River Oaks. The tree-shrouded streets and ivy-covered mansions had always seemed oppressive to Nina. She hated to think of her baby in such an atmosphere.

"What else did you find out?" she asked.

"Her husband, Clayton Baldwin, is vice president at Chambers Petroleum, which is owned by her father, a man named J. D. Chambers. Any of these names ring a bell?"

Nina frowned. "No. Should they?"

"From what I could gather, the Chambers family is pretty well connected in the petroleum industry, as well as in the River Oaks social circles. Thought you might have seen their names in the paper."

Nina took a deep breath, trying to quiet her racing heart. Something about Sergeant Farrell's tone worried her. "So what do we do next? When can we go confront Vanessa Baldwin? When can I get my baby back?"

"It's not quite as simple as that. We're not talking about any Tom, Dick or Harry here. These people have clout."

"So what are you saying?" Nina demanded. "Because they're rich and powerful, the law can't touch them?"

"I'm not saying that at all. I'm saying we have to proceed with caution. I'm saying you could be mistaken."

"I'm not." Nina could feel her anger building.

Why wasn't he listening to her? Why wasn't he trying to help her?

Why did the rich and powerful have all the advantages?

She gripped the telephone in her fist. "I know what I saw."

"Or is it what you *think* you saw? What you *wanted* to see? I'm looking at a picture of Vanessa Baldwin right now, and I have to tell you, Nina, she doesn't look a thing like the sketch the artist drew of Karen Smith from your description. The hair, the mouth. Even the shape of the face. Everything is different."

"Because she was wearing a disguise!" Nina exploded. "You're a detective, for God's sake. You must have seen this thing before. Look at the eyes. They're a dead giveaway."

After a slight hesitation, Farrell said, "Even if there is some resemblance, we still have one major problem. Why would a woman of Vanessa Baldwin's stature risk stealing a child? She's from a high-profile family. It would be next to impossible to pass someone else's baby off as hers."

Nina gritted her teeth. "I don't know how she pulled it off, but it's your job to find out. She has my baby, and I want to know what you're going to do about getting him back."

His voice was quiet when he spoke, as if her outburst hadn't registered. "Do you read the paper, Nina? The *Houston Herald?*"

She frowned at the change of subject. "Sometimes. Why?"

"Did you read it today?"

She'd glanced through it that morning while having her coffee. "I scanned it."

"There was a picture of Vanessa Baldwin in the society section this morning. You don't remember seeing it?"

"No, I don't," Nina said angrily. "And what's more, I resent all these questions. Shouldn't you be questioning *her?*"

"Isn't it possible you saw Vanessa Baldwin's picture without even being aware of it, and that's why you recognized her in the park? You'd just been holding her baby. You said yourself you felt some sort of connection with him. Then you see this woman, the baby's mother, who looks familiar to you, and you think she's Karen Smith. You *want* her to be Karen Smith."

Nina's heart thudded against her rib cage. How could he not believe her? What was she going to do?

"It was bound to happen sooner or later," he explained. "You go to that park every day hoping to find your baby, hoping to see Karen Smith, even though you've always known in your heart the odds were next to impossible."

"But not entirely impossible," Nina insisted. "Because I did see her."

"I keep coming back to the same question," Farrell said softly. "If Karen Smith and Vanessa Baldwin are one and the same, why would she go back to that park? Why would she risk being seen?"

"Dear God," Nina whispered. "You're not going to do anything about this, are you?"

"Nina—"

"You're *afraid* of them." A hysterical sob rose in Nina's throat, but she swallowed it back down. "The police won't touch them because of who they are. People like that can do anything they damn well please, and to hell with the rest of us. Is that it? Well, I'm not afraid of them. I'll get my baby back with or without your help.''

"Nina, listen to me," Farrell said urgently. "You've got to get a grip here, or you could find yourself in a lot of trouble."

His words echoed inside her. The man in the park had said the same thing to her. "*I* could be in a lot of trouble? What have I done?"

Farrell's voice hardened with warning. "Nothing yet, and I want to keep it that way."

"Don't worry about me," Nina said. "I can take care of myself."

"I wish I could believe that," he muttered. "Look, I'll do some checking, find out what I can about Vanessa Baldwin and her baby. But, Nina, this has got to be done on the q.t. I don't want harassment charges coming down on either of our heads, you got that? You stay away from Vanessa Baldwin, and for God's sake, whatever you do, stay away from that baby."

Chapter Four

"Oh, Mr. Chambers, it's you. You startled me." The nanny stopped in the nursery doorway when she saw Grant standing over John David's bed. She looked flustered by his presence, and not a little guilty.

She entered the room hesitantly, and Grant straightened from the crib, where he had been trying to quiet the baby. "He was crying when I came in, Mrs. Becker. No one was in here with him."

"Oh, please call me Alice," she said with a breathless little laugh. "I just stepped out for a minute. Has the party already started downstairs?" Her gaze checked out Grant's tuxedo, then quickly shifted to the crib, where John David was excitedly waving his arms and legs and blowing spit bubbles at his uncle with gusto.

"Actually I came a little early to see you," Grant told her.

Her hand flew to the neckline of her dress, where a dull red flush crept upward, giving her a feverish glow. "Oh! What about?"

"I wanted to talk to you about the incident in the park this afternoon."

"Oh." Her tone dropped and so did her hand. "That woman, you mean."

"Yes, exactly." Grant hadn't been able to get "that woman" out of his head. Something about her had seemed eerily familiar to him, and yet he was sure she'd been telling the truth when she said they'd never met. And when she'd assured him she meant John David no harm.

So why couldn't he forget her?

She was hardly the sort of woman who would capture a man's imagination. Her waiflike appearance was not the studied look of a fashion model, but rather that of a woman who had fallen on hard times. Her face had been too narrow to be striking, her features too nondescript to be memorable, and yet there had been something very unsettling about her, a sadness and desperation in her eyes that haunted Grant much like those of the begging children he'd seen in Third World countries. He wanted to put her out of his mind, and yet he couldn't. Because like those starving children, the woman in the park had possessed something very rare. A quiet dignity and purity of soul that no amount of money could ever buy.

Grant found himself wondering what had made those eyes seem far too old and experienced for her face.

The nanny shuddered delicately. "I don't mind telling you, she just about scared me to death. I don't know what I would have done if you hadn't shown up."

Grant shrugged. "I don't think she meant the baby any harm. At any rate, I doubt we'll ever see her again, so the whole episode is best forgotten. And that's what I wanted to talk to you about. Did you mention any of this to my sister?''

The woman hesitated, calculating, Grant suspected, the answer he wanted to hear. There was something about Alice Becker that didn't elicit his trust. He wondered just how thoroughly Vanessa and Clayton had checked out her references.

''I haven't mentioned it to Mrs. Baldwin yet,'' she finally admitted. ''I was waiting for the right time.''

''Good,'' Grant said. ''Because I don't want you to tell her at all.''

The woman's narrow brows rose in surprise. ''Why not?''

''You know about my sister's condition.'' It was a statement, not a question. His father had always insisted that anyone who came to work in the Chambers household be informed of Vanessa's heart problem so that if an emergency ever arose, the staff would know instantly how to handle it. Grant doubted that policy had changed since his sister had moved into her own home. J. D. Chambers wouldn't allow it. His daughter had to be protected, at all costs.

''There's no use upsetting my sister needlessly,'' he explained.

''But somehow I don't feel right keeping this from her.'' She slanted Grant a look, which wasn't hard to interpret. If Vanessa were to ever find out about the woman in the park, Alice Becker didn't want to be held accountable.

''Don't worry. I'll take full responsibility.'' Bending over the crib once more, Grant let his nephew capture one finger in his tiny fist for a long moment, then straightened. ''Good night, Mrs. Becker.''

The woman started to say something, perhaps to ask him again to call her Alice, but then she seemed to change her mind. She nodded and murmured, "Good night, Mr. Chambers," as her gaze took his measure one last time before he turned and strode from the room.

NINA SAT IN THE BACK of the taxi and stared out the window, but the passing scenery was nothing more than a blur. How could she focus on her surroundings when her thoughts were so chaotic?

Was she doing the right thing?

What if she got caught?

Catching a glimpse of her reflection in the window, she marveled at the changes in her appearance. She'd spent hours that afternoon at an exclusive uptown salon, being made over for tonight. The bill, along with the price of a new gown, had been staggering, but Nina knew the extravagance had been worthwhile.

Gone was the long, mousy blond hair, the pale complexion, the dull, pain-filled eyes. Her hair, cut short in a chic new style, shimmered with golden highlights, her complexion glowed with soft color and her green eyes sparkled with excitement. Nina hardly even recognized herself, and she told herself no one else would, either.

Resting her head against the back of the seat, she let her mind drift over the rest of the afternoon's events, searching—she suspected—for affirmation that she was doing the right thing. That she had covered all her bases.

After speaking with Sergeant Farrell for the second time, she'd fished the morning newspaper out of the trash and turned to the society section. Vanessa Baldwin's likeness had smiled up at her, and Nina's heart had plunged in disappointment. Either the picture was deceptive or she'd been mistaken in the park. Vanessa Baldwin looked nothing like Karen Smith.

Could Sergeant Farrell be right? Had Nina glimpsed something in Vanessa Baldwin's eyes only because she so desperately wanted to?

The accompanying article reported that Vanessa Baldwin was hosting a formal reception that night in her River Oaks home in honor of her brother, Grant Chambers, who had just returned from Venezuela. After reading the article, Nina had come up with a dangerous plan. For her own peace of mind, she had to get a closer look at Vanessa Baldwin. She had to be sure.

And if she was honest with herself, she had to admit she wanted to see the baby again, too, although she knew that would be the riskiest part of her plan.

Oh, but to hold that child in her arms again…to savor his sweetness…

Nina drew a long, shaky breath. Above all else, she had to remain rational. If Vanessa Baldwin wasn't Karen Smith, then her baby wasn't Dustin, and Nina would have no right to see him, let alone to hold him. She could not afford to lose sight of that fact.

The taxi pulled through the gates of the Baldwin estate and slowly wound its way around the semicircular driveway to stop in front of the Mediterranean-style mansion, blazing with lights. Nina glanced at the stucco facade and the wrought-iron balconies as she stepped out into the cool October air.

Another car had pulled up behind hers, and two

couples got out. Nina fell into step behind them, forcing herself to strike up a casual conversation with one of the women as they mounted the stairs and walked through massive oak doors into the grand foyer.

GRANT SAW HER IMMEDIATELY. He'd been talking with his father and several business associates about the Venezuelan project, but the moment she walked into the room, everyone else faded into the background.

She wasn't beautiful in the traditional sense of the word, but there was something about her, an elegance and quiet sophistication that made him think she would be an interesting woman to know.

The simple black gown she wore left her arms and shoulders bare, and revealed a body beneath the silky fabric that was more slender than Grant would ordinarily have found attractive. But rather than making her seem frail, her petite stature was surprisingly sensual. Womanly.

Drifting away from the people she'd come in with, she accepted a glass of champagne from one of the hovering waiters, then slipped unobtrusively into a corner, her gaze raking the crowded room. Grant watched her over the rim of his own glass. Had they met before? He didn't think so, and yet there was something intriguingly familiar about her. He excused himself and crossed the room toward her.

As he approached, Grant saw something flit across her features. Recognition? If he didn't know better, he would have almost sworn it was fear.

"I know this is going to sound like the worst kind of come-on," he said, "but have we met before?"

Her gaze flitted upward to his. She licked her lips nervously. "No. I'm sure we haven't."

"You look...not exactly familiar, but—" He paused, studying her features. "There's something about you."

"I...guess I just have one of those faces."

That wasn't it, but Grant didn't think it wise to pursue the topic any further. She looked a little skittish, as if she might turn and bolt at any moment. And he sure as hell didn't want that.

"I'm Grant Chambers." He extended his hand, and she accepted it only briefly before pulling her fingers from his grasp. When she made no move to introduce herself, he said, "And you are...?"

A look of panic flashed across her features. He couldn't imagine why she seemed so nervous in his presence. Was he that intimidating? He'd never thought so before.

"I'm—" She broke off, her gaze darting from his. He saw her take a deep breath, and then she said softly, "Actually I'm not supposed to be here."

"You mean you crashed my sister's party?" When she nodded, he laughed. That explained her nervousness. She probably thought he'd have her tossed out, but that was the furthest thing from Grant's mind.

He stared down at her, his interest piqued. A pulse beat in her throat, and he thought impulsively how exciting it would be to press his lips against the spot, to feel her soft, warm skin throbbing beneath his mouth.

Leaning toward her, he said, "Don't worry. Your secret's safe with me."

Her eyes widened in surprise. "Then…you don't mind my being here?"

"Hardly." Their gazes met once again before she quickly glanced away. Grant used the moment to study her as she turned to watch the crowd. He couldn't remember the last time he'd been so intrigued by a woman. "So, tell me. Any reason for crashing this particular party?"

She lifted her shoulders, a slight movement that brought Grant's gaze downward, to the creamy skin of her throat and the alluring shadow of cleavage at her neckline. He felt something tighten inside him.

"I came with my cousin." She nodded vaguely toward the center of the room.

Grant followed her gaze and said, "You mean Cynthia? I didn't know she had a cousin."

The woman bit her lip. "We're not that close. I don't see her very often."

"You don't live in Houston then?"

"I'm from…San Antonio."

"Really? I'm pretty familiar with the city. Where do you live?"

She hesitated again, as if debating whether she wanted him to know that much about her. Then she shrugged and named a neighborhood Grant knew very well. He lifted his brows in surprise. "Small world. I have a good friend who lives in Alamo Heights. We were roommates at UT. His name is Trent Fairchild. You don't, by chance, know him, do you?"

Something flashed across her features, setting off a warning inside Grant. Too late, he saw the champagne glass slip from her fingers and shatter against the marble floor at their feet.

Clasping a hand to her heart, she stared at the broken flute in horror. "Oh, my God."

Her face had grown so pale, Grant took her arm to steady her. "What's wrong? Was it something I said?"

"No. No, it wasn't that. I-it just…slipped from my fingers. I'm sorry," she stammered, as if she couldn't quite believe what had happened. "I'm usually not that clumsy."

"No problem. It's just a broken glass. Happens all the time." He motioned to one of the waiters, who hurried over to clean up the mess. Grant used the opportunity to pull her even farther away from the crowd.

She still looked shaken, and he wondered why such a trivial accident had caused her such concern. "Believe me, that glass will never be missed."

Her gaze swept the elegant room, and a brief shadow crossed over her features. "I'm sure it won't. But I *am* sorry."

"Accidents happen. So long as it wasn't the company that made you so nervous."

"Wh-what?"

Her green gaze seemed so guileless, Grant wondered if she could really be so innocent not to recognize his own clumsy attempts at flirtation. Was he that out of practice?

Or maybe she just wasn't interested. Maybe it was time to move on. There were a lot of important people at the gathering, and Grant knew he should be working the crowd—as his brother-in-law was undoubtedly doing. As his father would expect both of them to do. But try as he might, Grant couldn't muster up much enthusiasm for it at the moment.

He didn't mind talking about the Venezuelan project, which had turned out to be a very profitable venture, but a conversation about his return to the States always led to the inevitable speculation about his exile. And Grant didn't like thinking about the past. He didn't like remembering how closely he'd come to losing everything, and all because of a woman.

So why wasn't he being more cautious now? Why was he hell-bent on pursuing this woman when she so obviously didn't want to be pursued?

"Perhaps I should leave," she said, as if reading his mind.

Grant frowned. "Because of a broken glass?" When she shrugged helplessly, he said, "Look, if you feel that badly about it, there's only one thing you can do."

Her glance turned wary. "What?"

"Dance with me."

"Oh, I couldn't, I mean, I'm really not much of a dancer," she said in a rush.

"Why don't you let me be the judge of that?" He took her hand and felt it tremble in his. For some reason, it made her seem vulnerable and sweet. Qualities he'd always vastly underrated, he decided.

"But—"

"No 'but's," he insisted. "I have a feeling that at midnight you're going to disappear, and I'll never see you again. At least let me have one dance to remember you by."

IN HER WILDEST DREAMS, Nina could not have imagined such a strange scenario. When she'd seen Grant Chambers walking across the room toward her, she'd been sure he'd recognized her from the park and was coming to throw her out. Or maybe even have her arrested.

But then she'd seen the admiration in his gray eyes, and realized in a rush of relief that he had no idea who she was. Her makeover had worked, and she'd tried her best not to say or do anything to give herself away. But then he mentioned Trent Fairchild, and her reaction was instinctive. She thought for a moment she might actually pass out.

How ironic that she had come here searching for the truth about her baby only to end up in the arms of a man who was a friend of her worst enemy. Trent Fairchild had sworn he would find a way to make Nina pay for Garrett's death, and she couldn't help wondering again if he was somehow connected to Dustin's disappearance. Sergeant Farrell had cleared him months ago, but Nina had never been quite as certain.

"You're trembling." Grant's deep voice vibrated against her ear. "Are you cold?"

"A little." She tried to hold herself away from his body, but Grant Chambers would have none of that. He was a man used to getting his own way, and when he pulled her more tightly into his arms, there was little she could do to resist.

"Better?"

No! she wanted to scream, but all she could do was nod and let herself be drawn against him. He was very tall, towering over her in a way that made her feel a little too vulnerable, and he was darkly handsome in a way that would make most women's knees go weak. But Nina was immune to rich and powerful men. She didn't trust them. It had been her experience they almost always had a hidden agenda.

The only male she had any interest in at the moment was her son, and she would do whatever she had to in order to find him, even if it meant dancing with Grant Chambers. Even if it meant pretending an interest she didn't feel. For all Nina knew, her baby could be upstairs at this very moment, and Grant just might be the one person who could lead her to him.

"You lied to me, didn't you?"

His deep voice was like a caress against her ear. Nina felt her mouth go dry. "What do you mean?"

"You said you weren't much of a dancer. I knew that couldn't be true."

She laughed softly, a breathless release of nerves. "Just because I haven't stepped on your toes yet doesn't mean I won't."

"I'm not worried." He smiled down at her again, and Nina felt her breath catch in her throat. He really was a very attractive man. His gray eyes, hooded and sensual, were fringed with thick lashes and shadowed with just enough mystery to make a woman wonder where he'd been and what he'd seen. What he'd done and whom he had done it with.

He didn't look anything like his sister. Vanessa was blond and fair, and catching a glimpse of her in the crowd, Nina couldn't help wondering again if she'd made a tragic mistake. Could a black wig, glasses and the right makeup change a person's appearance so dramatically?

Just look at me, Nina thought. Grant Chambers had stared accusingly into her eyes only a few hours ago, and now here they were dancing.

"What are you so deep in thought about?" he asked her.

"I...was just thinking about your sister."

"Vanessa? What about her?"

"I heard she'd recently had a baby, but she looks so thin. I was wondering how she got her figure back so quickly."

"I wasn't around when she had the baby, but I imagine Vanessa did whatever was necessary. She's very much a perfectionist."

Something in his tone made Nina glance up at him. Did he suspect a dark side to his sister, as well? "She's very beautiful," Nina murmured. "Does the baby look like her?"

Grant considered the question for a moment. "I've never really given it much thought. Vanessa and Clayton are both fair, and what little hair John David has is dark. Come to think of it, I guess he looks a little more like me than he does either one of them." The notion seemed to please him.

"You surprise me," Nina tried to say lightly. "You don't strike me as the baby type."

He laughed. "I guess I surprise myself. I've never been around babies much. But there's something special about John David. It's hard to explain. He's just so—I don't know—innocent, I guess. He makes you want to protect him." His smile seemed self-deprecating. "Not exactly a manly thing to say, is it?"

On the contrary. Nina had a sudden vision of the way Grant had looked that afternoon when he'd taken the baby from her arms. His menacing presence had terrified her, and she'd had no doubt that he would do whatever necessary to protect the child.

There'd been no question of his masculinity then or now. He was not only a man used to getting what he wanted, but was also a man who would fiercely guard what he thought was his.

Nina shivered again, and Grant's arms tightened around her. "You're freezing," he said. "Let me go get your coat. What does it look like?"

Her mind raced. If she remained in Grant Chambers's presence for much longer, she'd surely give herself away. She had to get away from him. She had to find a way to get upstairs and locate the nursery.

"It's a very common style," she said. "You'd better let me go get it."

She tried to pull out of his arms, but he held her for an instant longer. His gaze deepened, letting her know in no uncertain terms that he found her attractive. And that he had every intention of acting on that attraction. Nerves fluttered along Nina's backbone.

"Promise me you'll come back," he demanded softly.

She hesitated, striving for poise. Then she nodded and walked away.

SLOWLY NINA CLIMBED the curving staircase, her heart pounding against her chest. *This is it,* a little voice whispered inside her. *The moment of truth.*

Soon she would find the baby they called John David and stare down into his little face. Soon she would know whether or not he was hers, because surely her instincts would tell her.

Pausing on the wide balcony, she glanced down at the throng below her, her gaze finding and resting on

Vanessa Baldwin. The woman hadn't given her a second glance all evening. She obviously had no idea who Nina really was or why she was there. Vanessa had no idea of the possible threat that lurked in her midst.

How easy would it be, Nina wondered daringly, to grab the baby and run? To simply disappear with him rather than letting the law take its course?

She had a little money put away. Though she'd received nothing from Garrett's massive trust fund, she'd been the beneficiary of a life-insurance policy he'd left behind. She could use that money now to go somewhere far away and make a new life for herself and her son. Far away from the Fairchilds and the Baldwins and the Chamberses.

But seeing Vanessa Baldwin tonight had only confused Nina more. Vanessa was so beautiful and elegant, so sure of herself. Karen Smith had been the total opposite, demure and shy and so painfully insecure. Had it all been an act, an elaborate charade to win Nina's confidence and then steal her baby?

Had Trent Fairchild played a part in the tragedy?

Had Grant?

Almost inadvertently, her gaze came to rest on Grant Chambers. He was talking to a woman in a red-beaded dress, and as Nina stood watching, she saw the woman place her hand on his arm, as if staking her claim. Uneasiness stirred inside Nina. A memory of something she'd read in the paper that afternoon came back to her. There'd been a vague reference to a scandal involving Grant four years ago before he'd moved to Venezuela. Though Nina hadn't paid much attention to it at the time, she wondered now what had happened to him. Why he'd felt compelled to leave the country back then.

If he'd been in Venezuela for the past four years as he'd told her when they were dancing—then he hadn't been here when Nina's baby had been born. He hadn't been anywhere near Galveston when Dustin had been stolen.

Why, all of a sudden, did she so desperately want to believe that? Nina wondered. Why did it matter if Grant was guilty or innocent so long as she found her baby?

As if sensing her scrutiny, he lifted his head suddenly and found her on the landing. Even from a distance, Nina could feel the intensity of his gaze, the power of his presence, and she shivered.

When he found out who she was, why she had come here, Grant Chambers would become her enemy. The notion left Nina oddly shaken, and only by sheer force of will was she able to tear her gaze from his and turn away.

THERE WERE SEVERAL DOORS that opened from the upstairs hallway, and Nina had no idea which one was the nursery or if the baby's room was even on this floor. She started checking the rooms one by one, knowing she had only a few moments before Grant would start to wonder what was taking her so long to find her coat and come looking for her.

Most of the rooms on the second floor were bedrooms, the largest of which was obviously the master suite. Nina paused in the hallway for a moment, glancing over her shoulder toward the stairway and the balcony that overlooked the large area below.

Satisfied that no one was about, she let herself into Vanessa Baldwin's sitting room.

And just what do you expect to find? Nina asked herself as she stood leaning against the door, her gaze scanning the room. *A dark wig? Black-rimmed glasses?*

If Vanessa Baldwin really was Karen Smith, she would have destroyed her disguise a long time ago. Searching her suite would be an exercise in futility, but Nina couldn't bring herself to leave. Not yet.

The sitting room was elegantly decorated in shades of cream, gold and dark green. Though it had been beautifully done, Nina found the room totally lacking in personality. There was nothing out of place, nothing that didn't match, nothing whatsoever that gave away anything of the personality of the woman who occupied these quarters.

As Nina turned to leave, a photograph on an antique cherry wood table caught her eye. She crossed the room and picked up the gold frame, her heart hammering inside her as she stared down at the image.

Here's your proof, a little voice taunted her. *This is what you came for.*

The woman in the picture was Vanessa Baldwin. A very beautiful and very pregnant Vanessa Baldwin. Standing in front of a building with white columns, she looked to be about seven or eight months along.

Nina's hands trembled as she stared down at the photograph. Did this confirm her doubts then? Did this prove Vanessa Baldwin wasn't Karen Smith?

Could Nina have wanted to find Karen so badly that she'd conjured her up in the park that afternoon? Had she so desperately wanted to believe the baby she'd held in her arms was Dustin that she'd managed to convince herself he was?

Sergeant Farrell had warned her. The odds were against her, the coincidences too great. But she'd refused to believe him.

Nina had never felt so near an emotional edge as she did at that moment. Not when Garrett had died and not even when Dustin had disappeared. She'd somehow managed to hold herself together in the face of those tragedies because she'd always been a survivor. She'd had to be.

But now.

Now Nina had to question her own sanity. She could no longer trust her own judgment.

Dear God, what if she had taken that baby? What if she had put someone else through the same hell she'd gone through when Dustin disappeared?

Nina closed her eyes as the strange room swayed around her. She had to get out of there before she said or did something that would get her carted off to jail or to an insane asylum or…worse.

Taking a steadying breath, she hurried across the room and opened the door, but just as she started to step into the hallway, she heard another door open. Stepping back into the room, Nina left the door slightly ajar so that she could see down the hallway. What if it was Vanessa? she thought, frantically casting about for a hiding place.

But then she saw someone come out of a room three or four doors down, and Nina smothered a gasp. She recognized the woman from the park, John David's nanny.

As Nina watched her, the woman took a flask from the pocket of her uniform and stared down at it for a moment. Then, lifting it to her lips, she took a long swallow and wiped her mouth with the back of her hand. Slipping the flask back into her pocket, she turned and headed down the hallway, away from what Nina thought might be the nursery.

Once the woman was out of sight, Nina left the room, pulling the door closed behind her. Hurrying down the hallway, she was almost past the nursery door when she heard sounds of distress coming from within.

Nina paused in spite of herself. A voice inside her screamed to get out of there as fast as she could, but the noises coming from inside the nursery drew her like a magnet. It didn't matter that she'd convinced herself only moments earlier the baby inside that room really was Vanessa Baldwin's, or that Nina's own sanity had been called into question.

This was a different matter entirely, she told herself. After what she'd just witnessed with his nanny, Nina had to make sure the baby was all right. She'd do the same for any child.

Opening the door wider, Nina slipped inside. The room was dimly lit with a night-light, but the curtains at the bay window had been left open, allowing in moonlight. The baby lay on his back in his crib, wide-awake and fussing as he tried to corral one foot toward his mouth.

Nina leaned over the bed and stared down at him. The baby instantly quieted. Rather than being alarmed at a strange face peering down at him, he seemed fascinated by her sudden appearance. He returned her stare for a long moment, then laughed out loud, thumping both heels against the mattress as he vied for her attention. Rolling on his stomach, he inched his way on hands and knees toward her.

"Oh, you precious," Nina whispered. She reached down to touch the sparse dark hair on his head.

With some difficulty, he maneuvered himself to a sitting position, lifting his arms for Nina to take him.

Who could have resisted such charm?

She picked him up and held him in her arms. Her teardrop earrings must have sparkled in the moonlight, for the baby laughed and grabbed for her ear.

Nina laughed, too, rescuing her earring just in the nick of time.

"You really are the sweetest little thing," she whispered. "Even if you aren't mine."

Reluctantly she returned him to his crib, and as if sensing her imminent departure, he wrinkled his little brow into a deep frown of displeasure.

And Nina froze.

Her heart almost stopped at that look.

Afraid to move, afraid even to glance away, she stared down at him, her breath suspended somewhere in her throat.

Something about the way he'd frowned at her, the way his little eyes had sobered with unhappiness…

For just a moment, for just an instant, Nina had seen Garrett staring up at her.

How many times had she seen that same look of unhappiness on her husband's face?

"Dear God," she whispered. "You *are* Dustin."

Without thinking of the consequences, without analyzing her actions, Nina reached for the baby again. But before she could lift him from the crib, a man's voice said from the doorway, "What are you doing in here?"

STILL IN SHOCK, Nina glanced up to find Grant staring at her from the doorway. Slowly he entered the room and walked toward her.

Nina's heart thundered in her chest. What should she do? Snatch the baby and make a run for it?

But even as the notion flitted through her mind, she realized how utterly insane that would be. They would never let her out of this house with Dustin. She had to remain calm and rational until she could get to a phone and call Sergeant Farrell. Now that she knew for certain this baby was hers, he would have to help her. He couldn't turn his back on her now.

"I—I was trying to find my coat," Nina stammered.

"In here?" Grant stood on the other side of the crib, staring at her in the moonlight.

Nina's mind raced. She glanced down at the baby, then back up at Grant. "I heard him crying. I just came in to see if anything was wrong."

Grant's brows drew together in a thunderous expression, a look that threatened to steal Nina's breath again. "Where is that woman?"

"You mean the nanny?" Nina managed to ask. "I saw her go downstairs. At least, I think it was her."

He muttered something else, something Nina couldn't make out, then he moved around the crib to stand beside her. His expression seemed to soften in the moonlight as he stared down at her. "I was beginning to think you weren't coming back."

She moistened her lips. "Well, I—"

He placed his hands on her shoulders. Nina tried to quiet her pounding heart, tried to steady her trembling legs. She had to get out of here, she thought frantically. She had to get to a phone and call Farrell.

Instead she gazed up at him, frozen in fear.

"Look, I know this probably sounds crazy. I don't even know your name," he said. "But I feel as if we have some sort of connection. I don't want to let you walk out of here tonight and never see you again."

Without warning, he bent and touched his lips to hers. If Nina hadn't already been in such a state of shock, she might have reacted more quickly. She might have been able to avoid the kiss, or even to push him away. But as it was, all she could do was stand there as waves of emotion crashed over her.

Her first thought was of Dustin, her second of Garrett. Their first kiss had been deeper, more passionate and yet...

Something stirred inside Nina. Something that couldn't be.

Breaking the kiss, she took a faltering step away from Grant. She could see his face in the moonlight. The dark, brooding eyes. The strong angle of his jaw and chin. The way he was looking at her.

That afternoon in the park, Nina had thought him the most formidable-looking man she'd ever seen. That opinion had only strengthened with his kiss.

"You're very beautiful," he murmured, drawing the back of his hand along her jawline.

"Please don't," she whispered.

"Don't what?" His dark gaze held her enthralled. "Don't touch you? Don't kiss you? Don't try to pursue you?"

All of those, she wanted to scream, but she heard

herself responding shakily, "It's…too fast…I can't think—"

"Sometimes it happens that way." His voice pulsed with sensuality. Dark and seductive, it promised to take Nina places she had no wish to go. "Sometimes you have no control."

"I don't believe that," she said.

One dark brow rose as his fingertip traced the strap of her gown. "You've never been swept away by passion? Never thrown caution to the wind?"

She'd thrown caution to the wind many times, Nina thought. When she'd married Garrett. When she'd come here tonight.

But swept away by passion?

In the crib beside them, the baby fretted. He'd rolled over on his stomach and was staring at them through the bars of the bed. Rather than breaking the tension of the moment, his soft baby sounds only added to the turmoil inside Nina. More than anything, she wanted to go to him and pick him up, tell him and the rest of the world that he was her son and she would always, always take care of him.

But she couldn't do that. Not yet. Not alone. Because in spite of that kiss, she only had to look into Grant Chambers's eyes to know that once crossed, he would be a terrifying adversary.

He laughed softly, a deep masculine sound that sent a shiver up Nina's spine. He leaned over and picked up the baby from the crib.

"What's the matter, buddy? Feeling left out?" Nina watched as Grant lifted the child over his head, and Dustin—John David—squealed with laughter.

It was easy to see that Grant was a doting uncle, and Nina wanted to take comfort in that fact. But how could she, when she had no way of knowing what his part in all this was? When she had no way of knowing what he would do when he found out who she really was?

He glanced at her and smiled. "Would you like to hold him?"

Nina's heart bounced against her chest. "Yes. Very much." She reached for the baby, but before her arms could close around his little body, the overhead light came on and she guiltily jumped back.

A gasp sounded from the doorway. Both Nina and Grant turned. The nanny stood just inside the room, her hand still on the light switch, her gaze fastened on Nina.

"You!" she screeched.

Nina's heart threatened to thrash its way out of her chest. What should she do now? Make a run for it? But how could she leave her baby, knowing what she knew about this woman? It made Nina's skin crawl to think of Dustin being entrusted to her care.

The nanny's hand left the light switch to point in Nina's direction. "You!" she squealed again.

"What the hell are you talking about?" Grant demanded. Reluctantly he returned the baby to the crib, then straightened to glare across the room at the nanny.

Her hair was all askew, her face flushed, her eyes bright and glassy. Nina watched in horror as she took several wobbling steps nearer.

Grant's gaze narrowed. "Good God," he said in disgust. "You've been drinking. I can smell it."

That stopped the nanny in her tracks. She weaved from side to side, her eyes squinting to focus, and for a moment, Nina thought—prayed—the woman would pass out. Then she seemed to gather whatever faculties she had left, and lifted her hand to stab at the air.

"It's her, Mr. Chambers! It's *her!*"

Grant cast a glance at Nina. "Have you two met?" he asked reluctantly. "Do you have any idea what she's babbling about?"

Nina put a hand to her throat. She still couldn't say a word. She shook her head.

The nanny stumbled toward her. "It's her! It's *her!* The woman from the park! Don't you recognize her, Mr. Chambers?"

Slowly Grant turned toward Nina again. She saw his expression in the moonlight, knew the moment when the truth dawned in his eyes.

"It *is* you."

"Oh, God! Oh, God!" the nanny wailed, clinging to the baby's crib. "Don't you see? She's come here to steal John David!"

The baby began to wail, too. Nina started toward him, but Grant's hand shot out and grabbed her arm. "Don't go near that baby."

His eyes were as cold and gray as steel, and Nina thought, *It's begun. Already he's becoming my enemy.* "Why did you come here tonight?" he demanded. "Who the hell are you?"

Nina hesitated, knowing it was only a matter of time before he found out the truth about her. He might as well hear it from her. She took a deep breath and met his gaze. "My name is Nina Fairchild," she said softly. "And I came here to get my baby."

Chapter Five

"I don't understand," Vanessa said weakly. "How did she get in?"

"Apparently she just walked in." Grant paced his sister's room. Even though he'd had almost an hour to try to put the pieces together, he still couldn't believe how easily he'd been duped by Nina Fairchild.

Fairchild. The name echoed inside his head. Garrett Fairchild's widow. No wonder she'd been so upset when he'd mentioned Trent. She must have been afraid she'd be discovered before she could carry out her plan.

And what exactly *was* her plan? he wondered. What the hell had she meant when she said she'd come here to get her baby? What on earth had possessed her to think John David was hers? Because she'd held him briefly in the park that afternoon? Was she *that* demented?

Grant glanced at his sister, who was lying in bed, a damp cloth across her forehead. Unfortunately Vanessa had walked in on the scene in the nursery before Grant had had time to get to the bottom of Nina's strange announcement. Alice Becker—the drunken fool—had blabbered hysterically to Vanessa about seeing Nina in the park that afternoon and how she'd tried to take John David then, how she'd come back tonight to finish the job.

Vanessa had taken one look at Nina and collapsed. While Grant had administered her heart medication, Alice Becker had taken it upon herself to call the police. Then she'd gone downstairs to alert Grant's father and Clayton, who had both rushed into the nursery with righteous fury blazing.

Grant hadn't had a minute alone with Nina after that. Everything had happened so quickly, and he'd been preoccupied with trying to make sure Vanessa was all right. But he'd caught a glimpse of Nina, tiny and forlorn looking while she stood near John David's crib, as he'd lifted his sister from the floor and carried her to her room. By the time he'd returned, the police—no doubt after his father had thrown around his considerable weight—had taken Nina away, leaving dozens of unanswered questions.

Vanessa's hand fluttered to her heart. "I don't understand. Who is she? What does she want?"

"Obviously a nut case," J. D. Chambers boomed from where he stood by the window. His dark brows drew together as he turned to stare at his daughter. "Don't you worry, princess. I'll take care of her. I'll take care of everything."

Clayton, icy blue eyes raking Grant with scorn, echoed his father-in-law's sentiments. "Yes, Van, darling. Don't worry about any of this. I've ordered extra security guards to watch the grounds tonight. There's no way she can get to the baby."

J.D. nodded approvingly, but Vanessa seemed less than reassured. She clutched Grant's hand. "Grant, what if she keeps claiming my baby is hers? What if the police believe her?''

Grant squeezed his sister's fingers in reassurance. ''Why would they believe her? She's obviously a very disturbed woman.'' But even as he said the words, an image of Nina Fairchild's sad, wise eyes materialized in his mind. She hadn't seemed troubled at all to him earlier. Could he have been that taken in by her?

''I don't know what I'd do if I lost John David.'' Vanessa's voice trembled with emotion. She looked more frail than Grant had seen her in a long time.

''Look, there's no way she can take John David away from you,'' Grant said. ''You're his mother. You gave birth to him. Not that it will ever come to this, but you have his birth certificate. Your doctor has records.''

Vanessa gasped. ''Oh, God. It won't go that far, will it? I couldn't stand it—''

''Hell, no, it won't go that far,'' J.D. thundered. ''If I have anything to say about it, that woman will be put in a loony bin, where she belongs. Where she can't hurt my little girl.'' He walked over and patted Vanessa's head, as if she were still a child.

Vanessa looked up at her father. ''Please don't let that woman make trouble for me, Daddy.''

''That woman's troublemaking days are over,'' J.D. promised with a grand sweep of his hand. ''What we have to make sure of now is that no one else gets wind of this. The Ventura merger is in a precarious stage right now. If they were to hear of another scandal brewing—'' His accusing gaze landed on Grant for a moment, then shifted back to Vanessa. ''But that's not anything for you to worry about, princess. You get some rest now. We'll take care of everything, won't we, boys?''

"Of course we will," Clayton readily agreed. He bent to kiss Vanessa's forehead. "Rest now, like your father said."

"Come on," J.D. ordered. "We need to talk."

He and Clayton went out into the hallway, but when Grant would have followed, Vanessa clung to his hand. "I know Daddy and Clayton mean well, but it's you I've always been able to count on, Grant. You're my big brother. You've always been there to protect me."

"I'm still here," he said, wishing she didn't look quite so pale.

"Remember that time when I was twelve and you and Riley Addams were sixteen, and he tried to kiss me while he thought you weren't looking? You punched him so hard you broke his nose. His mother spent a fortune on plastic surgery and sent the bill to Daddy. He was furious with you, but you never would tell him why you hit Riley. You said it had been taken care of, and there was no use talking about it. Remember?"

"I remember."

"You knew I'd egged Riley on, didn't you? You knew I'd asked him to kiss me."

Grant shrugged. "You were just a kid. Riley should have known better."

"The point is," Vanessa said softly, "you've always been there for me, even when I wasn't the good little girl Daddy always thought me. Even when I wasn't a princess."

Where was all this leading? Grant worried. "Vanessa—"

She clutched his hand as a tear slipped from her eye and ran down her ashen face. "Please, Grant. Don't let that woman anywhere near John David, no matter what she says. If anything were to happen to my baby, I don't think my heart could take it. If I lost him, I think I'd just up and die."

J.D. WAS PACING the hallway when Grant came out of Vanessa's room. He stopped and glared at his son. "We've got a serious situation on our hands here. Very serious."

"So it would seem."

"That woman has to be stopped."

"There's not much she can do from jail," Grant argued. He tried to picture Nina behind bars, but the image was too disconcerting. Everything about that woman was too damn confusing.

"I think we're okay for the moment," J.D. agreed. "That Becker woman did one thing right. She led the police up the back way. Nobody downstairs knows what happened, but if one of us doesn't get back down there and do some PR on the Ventura people, the merger could blow up in our faces. We could stand to lose millions."

"I'll go," Clayton eagerly volunteered. He started for the stairs, but J.D. stopped him.

"No, you won't. You stay with your wife, make sure nothing else upsets her tonight. I'll go down and talk to the Ventura people. And you—" he turned to Grant "—you get down to the police station, talk to that fruitcake. Find out what she wants, what her price is." His father's gaze narrowed on Grant. "I don't care what you have to do to get her to drop this nonsense."

"I CAN'T BELIEVE you went there after I specifically told you to stay away from Vanessa Baldwin and her baby. What do I have to do to get through to you?" Sergeant Farrell glared at Nina across the wooden table in the interrogation room where she'd been ushered a few minutes earlier.

She still couldn't forget that moment of absolute panic when she'd been recognized, the utter despair she'd experienced when she'd had to leave her son behind, the humiliation she'd felt at being handcuffed and hauled down to the police station like a common criminal. And then had come the slow, terrifying realization that there was no one she could call. No one who could help her. She didn't even know the names of any attorneys.

And so she'd used her phone call to reach the one man who at least knew what was going on. She stared at Sergeant Farrell and thought, *He probably wishes he'd never given me his home phone number.*

"Why did you do it, Nina? Why did you go there tonight?"

She rubbed her forehead with her fingertips. "You know why I went. I had to."

Farrell sighed heavily. "Do you have any idea how much trouble you're in?"

"They haven't charged me with anything yet," Nina said shakily. "Is that legal?"

"They can hold you for twenty-four hours. After that—"

"Twenty-four hours!" she cried. "I can't stay here that long. I have to get out of here. I have to get my baby."

"Nina—"

"Look, I know you don't believe me, but I *know*

that baby is Dustin. I saw him tonight. I held him again.'' She reached across the table and clutched Farrell's arm. "He looks too much like my dead husband not to be his son."

Sergeant Farrell studied her for a long moment, then shrugged. "I give up. I don't know what to do anymore, how to get through to you. How can I make you understand that you can't simply make an accusation like that and have people believe you? You can't claim a baby is yours and expect the police to go in there and get him for you."

"What am I supposed to do, then?" Nina asked desperately. "Tell me, please. I'll do anything."

His mouth tightened. "That's what I'm afraid of. Look, I know how tough these past few months have been on you. A weaker person would have cracked a long time ago."

She stared at him in horror. "Is that what you think? You think I'm crazy?"

"I didn't say that. But you have been under an enormous strain. Maybe I can talk to the Baldwins, explain your situation to them. Maybe they'll decide not to press charges."

"And then what?" Nina asked angrily.

"Then you go home and forget this ever happened. Somehow you've got to find a way to get on with your life. Because if you don't—" He paused. "I don't have any jurisdiction up here, you know. The arresting officer let me see you out of professional courtesy. If this happens again, I won't be able to help you. You understand?"

Perfectly, she thought bitterly. He'd stuck his neck out for her once, but she wouldn't be able to count on him again.

Could she really blame him? It *was* a far-fetched story, and Sergeant Farrell had his career to think of, his own family to worry about. He couldn't risk his job because of her. She couldn't expect him to.

From now on, she was on her own. There was no one to believe her, no one to help her, no one who even cared. If Nina was going to get her baby back, she would have to find a way to do it herself.

The door to the interrogation room opened, and an officer stuck his head in. Farrell got up and went over to the door to converse with him in low tones. After a few minutes, the officer left and Farrell came back over to Nina.

"You're free to go," he said.

Relief flooded over her. "Does that mean the police believe my story?"

"It means Vanessa Baldwin and her husband aren't pressing charges against you. They've asked HPD to let you go."

Nina's relief turned to uneasiness. "Why?"

"I don't know, but if I were you, I'd consider it a gift." Farrell's gaze hardened. "Take my advice, Nina. Go home and forget this ever happened. Let me handle the investigation into Dustin's disappearance."

"Will that investigation include Vanessa Baldwin?" she demanded.

"You're not going to give up on this, are you?"

She met his gaze. "Would you?"

He shook his head. "You're headed for more trouble, Nina. Bad trouble. And there's not a damn thing I can do to help you."

GRANT SAW HER the moment she came out of the police station. It had started to drizzle while she'd been inside, and he watched from the warm interior of his car as she pulled her coat tightly around her and began walking down the street, presumably to find a cab.

He started his car and followed her, rolling his window down when he drew even with her. "Get in."

When she saw who he was, she pulled her coat even more tightly around her and glanced over her shoulder, as if to assure herself they were still within screaming distance of the police station. She said nothing, but kept walking.

Grant stopped his car and got out. When she saw him, she began running, her high heels echoing plaintively against the sidewalk. He caught her easily, but when he reached out to stop her, she stumbled away from him.

"Look, I'm not going to hurt you," he said.

"What do you want?" She was beginning to have a drowned-puppy look about her. Her short hair hung in damp clumps around her face, and her mascara was badly smeared from the rain or from crying, or both. For the first time that evening, Grant glimpsed the same desperation in her eyes he'd witnessed in the park that afternoon. But he also saw the same quiet dignity that made her throw back her shoulders and look him straight in the eye.

"Get in the car," he directed. "I'll give you a ride home."

"Why?"

"Look, if it wasn't for me, you'd still be inside there," he said in frustration, nodding toward the police station. "The least you owe me is an explanation."

Her gaze faltered, as if she was trying very hard not to break down. "You won't believe me," she said quietly.

"Why don't you try me?"

She glanced away, wiping her face with her fingertips. Grant saw that her hands were trembling badly, and for some reason, he couldn't help feeling sorry for her. She was obviously a disturbed woman, but what had made her so desperate?

"Why do you think my sister's baby is yours?"

She dragged her fingers through her damp hair. "Why should I tell you anything? You're one of them."

A bit of paranoia mixed with desperation, Grant thought. "'Them' who?"

She turned and started walking back toward the police station. "I'll call a cab," she muttered.

"I'll take you home," he said. "I promise I won't hurt you."

She stopped, obviously weighing her choices. Grant could understand her hesitation. Once free, walking back inside that police station would not be an easy thing to do, even if the alternative was accepting a ride with him.

"What did you mean when you said if it wasn't for you I'd still be in there?" she asked suddenly.

"I persuaded them to release you. And I've talked to my sister and her husband. They won't be pressing charges against you."

She stared up at him suspiciously. "Why not?"

He shrugged. "We all feel this is some sort of

misunderstanding. I think if we can just sit down and talk, we can get everything all cleared up.''

"Do you?"

The hardness in her voice took him by surprise. Maybe she wasn't quite as vulnerable as he'd thought. "What have you got to lose by talking to me?"

"I don't know." She clutched her coat like a lifeline. "That's what I've been trying to figure out."

GRANT PULLED HIS CAR onto the driveway of Nina's west-side bungalow and killed the engine. For a moment, all was silent inside the car. The drizzle had turned to a steady downpour after they'd left downtown, and the wind picked up, scattering leaves across her tiny front yard like bits of colored confetti. Her house was completely dark. It seemed cold and lonely compared to the leathery warmth of Grant's car.

But the coziness was only an illusion. Nina clutched the door handle, turning to study Grant's profile in the dim light from the streetlamp. He was staring at her house with a kind of brooding frown that made her heart trip inside her. What was he thinking? What was he planning? Did he, too, notice how dark her house was? How all alone she was?

Nina opened the door to get out, but his hand snaked out to snare her wrist. "We're not through yet."

"I think maybe we are," she said, forcing a steadiness to her tone she was far from feeling.

"I'm not leaving until you tell me why you came to my sister's house tonight. Why you think her baby is yours."

"Please," Nina whispered. "You're hurting me."
He wasn't. He was barely holding her, but she was desperate to be free of him.

"Sorry." Instantly his hand dropped from her wrist. Nina used the opportunity to bolt from the car and run for the house. She heard Grant get out, too, and by the time they reached the shelter of her front porch, both of them were soaked.

He didn't touch her again, but he might as well have. He stood in front of her, blocking her path of escape. Raindrops glistened in his dark hair, and though she could barely make out his features, she knew that his eyes were dark with anger, his expression grim with determination.

"Would you rather talk to the police again?"

He had her and Nina knew it. The thought of spending the night in jail terrified her. "All right," she said wearily. "Come inside, then."

She unlocked the door and stepped into the tiny foyer, reaching for the light switch as she shrugged out of her wet coat. Her gown was still relatively dry, but the bareness of her arms and neck made her feel too exposed. "I'll get you a towel," she said, not looking at Grant. But she could feel his gaze on her as she hurried through the living room into the darkened hallway beyond.

Retrieving a bath towel from the linen closet, she tossed it to Grant where he remained by the front door. Then she locked herself in her bedroom and shimmied out of the black gown, drawing on in its place a pair of jeans and a soft cotton sweater. Toweling her hair dry, she sat on the edge of the bed, contemplating her next move.

If she stayed inside her bedroom, refused to come

out, would he go away? She didn't think so. Grant Chambers seemed like a man who, once he had his mind set, would not easily give up.

Her only alternative was to go out there and tell him the truth. Tell him what his sister had done. Would he believe her? Not much chance of that, either, Nina thought, but a tiny part of her couldn't help hoping that he would. That Grant might turn out to be the ally she so desperately needed.

Because in spite of the fact that he was Vanessa Baldwin's brother, in spite of the fact that he was rich and powerful, handsome and charismatic, a man used to getting his own way, there was also something else about him that Nina couldn't quite define. It would be stretching it to call him vulnerable, and yet strangely enough, beneath his imposing facade, Nina had glimpsed an uncertainty about him earlier when he'd told her he didn't want her to disappear from his life.

Had that been nothing more than a come-on? Had the gentleness of his kiss been nothing more than an act?

Crossing the room, Nina unlocked the bedroom door and stepped quietly into the hallway. Pausing for a moment, she watched him prowl her living room, his dark expression and towering presence about as far removed from vulnerable as one could imagine.

Taking a deep breath, she walked into the living room to confront him.

Chapter Six

He turned when she entered the room, and Nina saw a subtle change in his expression as his gaze swept over her. Her hair was still damp, and her face had been wiped clean of makeup. She had an idea of what he was thinking.

"I look more like the woman you saw in the park this afternoon, don't I?"

"You cut your hair," he said noncommittally.

Nina drew her fingers through the short strands. "Cut it, got highlights, a professional makeup job. Amazing what they can do, isn't it?"

His features darkened. "It almost worked. You certainly had me fooled."

"Yes, but not the baby's nanny. She recognized me immediately."

He gave a short laugh, one without humor. "Even in her condition, she saw more than I did."

Nina bit her lip. "I saw her drinking earlier, before you came upstairs. I'm worried about the baby being in her care."

"Don't be. She'll be gone by morning." He dismissed the woman without so much as batting an eye.

Nina shivered, wondering if she would be next. If she would be taken care of that easily.

"What would have happened if she hadn't recognized you?" Grant asked. "What were you planning to do?"

Nina turned away, unable to meet his gaze. She walked over to the window and stared out into the rainy darkness. "I'm not sure."

He remained silent for a long moment, then said, "I don't understand why you think John David is your son. My sister gave birth to him."

"Do you know that for a fact?" Nina turned from the window to face him.

"I wasn't present when he was born, if that's what you mean. But there are records, doctors and nurses who witnessed his birth."

"Are you sure about that?"

When he didn't answer right away, Nina averted her gaze back to the window. She knew how bizarre this all sounded, how crazy she must seem to him, but the truth was the truth. The baby he called John David was her son. She had no more doubts. Not after tonight. Not after she'd seen his little face.

"May I sit?" Grant asked.

Nina shrugged. "I'm sorry. Of course. Please." She motioned toward the sofa, but made no move to join him.

After another long pause, he said, "You're Garrett Fairchild's widow, aren't you?"

Almost without realizing it, Nina folded her arms across her chest in a manner that was unmistakably defensive. "Yes. Did you know Garrett?"

"Not well. I met him a few times when I went to see Trent." His gaze met hers. "I was surprised to hear he'd gotten married. I never thought he was the type.''

''What do you mean?''

His brows lifted slightly. ''You've heard the expression 'mama's boy'?''

Nina gasped. ''What an unkind thing to say.''

''I'm sorry.'' But he didn't look at all contrite. ''I don't mean to hurt your feelings, but the truth is, I never cared much for Garrett.''

''But you liked Trent.'' Nina was hard-pressed to keep the disgust from her voice.

''I take it from your tone that you and he didn't get along.'' Grant watched her from the sofa, his eyes deep and brooding.

''You could say that.'' Nina lifted her chin. ''The fact is, he despised me.''

''Why?''

''Because I married his brother. Because I wasn't good enough to be a Fairchild.''

A brief frown flickered across Grant's features. ''That was it?''

''That was enough. People like the Fairchilds don't need more of a reason. I wasn't their kind. It was as simple as that.''

''Things are rarely that simple,'' he said in a sarcastic tone.

''No?'' She studied him for a moment. ''What about you? I'll bet you didn't give me a second thought this afternoon after you left the park. But tonight, dressed the way I was dressed, looking as if I belonged in your world, you—'' She broke off, suddenly embarrassed.

His eyes deepened in challenge. ''Supposing I told you you were wrong. Supposing I told you that I did give the woman in the park a second thought. More than a second. Supposing I told you I couldn't get her out of my mind. That there was something about her eyes…'' He rose and came to stand beside Nina at the window. Nerves fluttered in her stomach as he gazed down at her. ''I can't believe I didn't recognize you tonight, but then—'' It was his turn to stop, as if realizing he just might be going a little too far, revealing more of himself than he wanted to.

He turned and took a few steps away from her, changing the focus of the conversation back to her. ''What about Garrett's mother? How did you get on with Edwina?''

''I only met her once, at Garrett's funeral.''

His gaze turned skeptical at that. ''You only met her once? How long were you married?''

''A little less than a year. Look.'' Nina gestured impatiently with her hand. ''Why are you asking all these questions? Why does any of this matter?''

''It matters because I'm trying to understand you,'' he said.

''Why? So you can figure out how to make me go away?'' Nina asked angrily. ''Is that it? Is that why you're here? Were you the one assigned to take care of this nasty little problem?''

Impossibly Nina thought she saw a faint blush touch his cheeks. He shrugged. ''Believe it or not, I'd like to help you.'' When she made no move to reply, he said a little too carefully, ''I heard about Garrett's death. You must have been devastated.''

''He and I were in the process of getting a divorce at the time of his death.'' Nina wasn't looking at Grant, but she could sense his surprise and it gave her a perverse sense of satisfaction. She could almost read his mind. If Garrett's death hadn't driven her over the edge, then what had? What had made her come unglued and claim another woman's baby was hers?

Nina understood his motives all too well, but strangely enough, she found herself willing to talk, willing to try to make him understand.

"Garrett was killed in a car accident, wasn't he?" Grant prompted gently.

"It was raining that night," she said, almost to herself. Nina watched a raindrop trickle down the windowpane in front of her. "We'd just finished a meeting with the lawyers, and I'd gone storming out of the building. Garrett followed me. We had a terrible fight."

"Over the settlement?"

She almost smiled. "You would think that." She studied her reflection in the window, seeing the thin face, the hollow eyes, the bleak expression that had stared back at her since that night. "As a matter of fact, it *was* over the settlement, but not the way you mean. I didn't want anything from him. I'd brought nothing to the marriage, and I intended to leave the same way, but Garrett wouldn't have that. He needed to assuage his conscience, you see, and at the same time, buy me off so that I would leave town and not be an embarrassment to him or his family in the future."

Nina closed her eyes, remembering how hurt she'd been by Garrett's offer, how angry she'd been at the lies he'd believed about her.

"I just wanted to get away from all that ugliness," she said. "I wanted to go home and forget all the terrible lies his mother and brother had told him about me, all the things Garrett believed about me. But he wouldn't let me go. He got in the car with me, and I drove off to spite him." Impatiently she shoved her hair back from her face. "I was upset and not paying attention to the road like I should have been. And we kept arguing."

Nina, look out! Garrett's last words rang in her ears.

She gazed out the window, watching the rain, seeing the car plunge down the embankment, feeling the impact as it crashed into a tree. Remembering the moment when she realized Garrett was dead.

"There was blood everywhere," she said numbly. "I didn't know what else to do but go for help. When I came back—"

Grant's dark eyes were unexpectedly warm when she looked at him. "Did he know you were pregnant?"

She stared at him in surprise.

He shrugged. "Stands to reason you must have had a baby yourself recently if you think John David is yours."

"Six months ago," she answered. "His name is Dustin."

"What happened?"

Her heart tightened in grief. "That's a long story, too."

"I've got all night." Grant loosened his bow tie and took it off, slipping it into the pocket of his tuxedo jacket, then unfastening the top two buttons of his shirt. Nina watched, mesmerized by the movement of his fingers. Somehow the action seemed to calm her. "Did the Fairchilds know you were pregnant?"

"Not at first," she admitted. "I didn't know it myself until after I'd moved to Houston."

"Why did you come here? Why did you leave San Antonio?"

"Because they didn't want me there," she said bitterly. "Because they blamed me for Garrett's death, and Trent promised he'd find a way to make me pay. And I knew he could do it. I thought it was better for everyone if I left town and forgot I ever knew them."

"And then you found out you were pregnant."

Nina nodded. "I called the house to tell them. In spite of everything, I thought they had a right to know, but when I told Trent—" She broke off, shivering, remembering the conversation she'd had with her brother-in-law.

Forget it, Nina. You didn't get any money from my brother when he was alive, and you're not getting any now that he's dead.

Even if you are *pregnant, how do we know the baby is Garrett's?*

I'm warning you. Don't try to make trouble. And don't call here again.

"Trent made it clear they didn't want anything to do with me or my baby," she said.

"Because you and Garrett were divorcing at the time of his death?" Grant's question was softly spoken, but Nina sensed an undercurrent of something she didn't like.

"I know what you're thinking," she said coolly. "If my husband and I were getting a divorce, how did I become pregnant?"

"I know how you became pregnant," he said

dryly. "But I guess I am wondering about your relationship with Garrett."

Her failed marriage was not something Nina liked to dwell on, but she knew Grant wouldn't leave until he had what he'd come for. "After the divorce proceedings began, both Garrett and I had second thoughts. We tried to reconcile. I really thought we could make a go of it, but his family wouldn't leave us alone. In the end, he chose them over me. It was as simple as that."

"It doesn't sound simple at all," Grant said. "Especially the part about them not wanting anything to do with your baby."

It was Nina's turn to shrug. "Believe it or not, I was relieved. I wasn't afraid to raise my baby on my own. I've been alone all of my life."

"You don't have any family?" His gaze probed her face, and too late Nina realized the trap she'd fallen into. She had just admitted to Grant Chambers that she had no one in her life, no one to turn to for help. He and his family could do anything they wanted to her, and there would be no one to stop them.

No one but herself, she thought angrily. If they thought they could push her around, as the Fairchilds had, they were sadly mistaken. She'd grown up a lot in the past few months. Despite the fact that she was only twenty-six, Nina knew she could survive anything. She wasn't afraid of Grant Chambers. The sooner he realized that, the better.

"I do have family," she said. "I have my son."

Grant started to say something, then seemed to think better of it. He was still humoring her, Nina thought. Still treating her with kid gloves so she wouldn't go off the deep end.

That's fine. So long as I know I'm not crazy.

"Tell me about your pregnancy," he said. His gaze shifted subtly, dropping to her flat stomach, and Nina knew he was thinking the same thing about her that she'd thought about Vanessa. She looked too thin to have had a baby so recently, but the strain of Garrett's death and Dustin's disappearance had taken a toll.

"My pregnancy was normal," she said, almost defiantly. "I had a fairly easy time of it." Except for the fact that her husband was dead and her in-laws hated her.

"You had the baby here in Houston?"

Nina hesitated. Should she tell him everything? He was bound to find out sooner or later, especially if she was to take his sister on in court. A clever attorney would uncover every aspect of Nina's life, some of which she would rather leave hidden. There was really no reason why she shouldn't tell Grant herself.

And maybe, just maybe, she might be able to get him on her side.

Don't kid yourself, Nina.

"I had the baby in Galveston," she told him. "When I was in the third trimester, my obstetrician moved his practice there. It was very important to me that my baby not be delivered by a stranger, so I rented a small, furnished apartment on the island to be near him. But as it turned out, there was a terrible accident on the causeway bridge the night I went into labor. Dr. Bernard was held up for hours. A resident on duty at the hospital delivered Dustin."

"Your baby was born...healthy?"

She glanced at him sharply. "Meaning was he born alive? Did I become unhinged because of his death?"

He had the grace to look uncomfortable. "All right, yes. I guess that's what I'm asking."

"Dustin was born perfectly healthy. I held him in my arms. I nursed him. He was the most beautiful baby I'd ever seen," she said, fighting back tears.

"What happened to him, Nina?"

Wiping her face with her hands, she walked away from the window, turning her back on Grant. "There was a fire that night. The hospital was evacuated. They told me Dustin had been taken to St. Mary's here in Houston with all the other newborns. I was transferred, too, but when I got to the hospital, they couldn't find my baby. They thought it was a mix-up at first, but then—" She faltered.

Her back was still to Grant, but she sensed him moving toward her, and tensed. When he didn't try to touch her, Nina let out a long breath. "They never found him. The police concluded that someone had taken him during the confusion of the evacuation. I've always thought the fire was started as a diversion."

"My God," he said. "Who would do such a thing?"

Nina turned to face him, her expression grim. "There was a young woman I met in the park before Dustin was born. Her name was Karen Smith. We became friends. I think she may have...stalked me with the intent of stealing my baby."

Grant's brows drew together in a deep scowl.

"And you think this woman gave or sold your baby to my sister?"

"Not exactly."

He looked perplexed. "Then what? What do you think is this woman's connection to my sister? Why do you think Vanessa's baby is yours?"

Nina replied without hesitation. "Because I think that woman *was* your sister. I think Vanessa Baldwin and Karen Smith are one and the same."

GRANT STARED AT NINA helplessly, not knowing what to say. She didn't look crazy. She didn't sound insane. And yet the story she'd just told him was about as strange and bizarre as any he could imagine.

And the scary part was, Nina believed it. She was convinced it was true. Grant could see the conviction in her eyes, along with the grief and pain she'd endured for so long. First to have lost her husband, and then her baby—no wonder she was desperate for answers.

But to believe John David was her son. To think that Vanessa would have stalked her to steal her baby—

The only possible explanation was that grief and despair had sent Nina over the edge. But looking at her now, seeing the steely determination in her eyes, sensing the courage she'd mustered to face him, Grant found it impossible to accept that explanation. Nina Fairchild was perfectly sane.

It was the situation that was so crazy.

"Why would my sister steal your baby?" Grant asked her. "She had her own son."

"I don't think she did," Nina said. "I've thought about this a lot since seeing her in the park this af-

ternoon, and I've come up with two possible explanations—Vanessa was never pregnant and for some
reason desperately wanted a baby, or else she lost
her own baby and couldn't accept it.''

Grant stared at her in disbelief, his anger stirring
for the first time that night. ''How can you jump to
conclusions like that? You don't know anything
about my sister.''

Nina's chin lifted. ''I know she has my child.''

''Stop saying that, for God's sake. It can't be true.
There's no way.''

''Then how do you explain the fact that the baby
looks exactly like my dead husband?'' Nina asked
him. ''I saw him tonight. I held him in my arms. I
know that baby is mine.''

Her gaze grew even more defiant, and the thought
crossed Grant's mind that he and his family could
have an even bigger problem than they'd first
thought. It was obvious Nina wasn't going to go quietly away. Unless he could somehow manage to convince her that John David wasn't her baby, she could
make a lot of trouble for all of them, but especially
for his sister. Vanessa didn't need that kind of stress.
Her heart might not be able to take it.

He rubbed the back of his neck. ''Tell me about
this woman in the park.''

Nina shrugged. ''There isn't much to tell. She
sought me out, and we became friends. Then before
my baby was born, she said she and her husband
were reconciling and moving away. I never saw her
again. But a nurse saw a woman at the hospital the
night my baby was born who matched her description. She claimed she was my sister.''

"And you're saying this woman looked like *my* sister?" he asked skeptically.

Nina hesitated. "Not exactly. I mean…she was wearing a disguise. A dark wig and glasses. The police were never able to find Karen Smith. It was as if she vanished from the face of the earth. And then today, when I saw Vanessa in the park, I realized why. Because there never was a Karen Smith."

"You must know how all this sounds."

"I know it sounds crazy," Nina admitted. "I know you don't want to believe me. I wouldn't, either, if I were you. But it's true. Your sister stole my baby."

For a moment, Grant wanted to argue, but then he relented. "All right, look. This is getting us nowhere fast. Let's just put all our cards on the table, shall we? What exactly can I do to convince you that John David *isn't* your baby?"

Nina's eyes flashed with unexpected fire. "Nothing. I know that he is."

"But that isn't acceptable," Grant told her. "You've left no room to negotiate."

"Negotiate?" She stared at him with open disgust. "This is my baby we're talking about."

"And my sister's baby," he said grimly. "So let me put it another way. What exactly do you plan to do?"

That seemed to stop her for a moment. She wavered uncertainly.

He pressed his advantage. "You do have a plan, I assume. Short of kidnapping my nephew."

For the first time that night, she seemed rattled, unsure of herself. "This has all happened so quickly.

I haven't thought what to do beyond finding out for certain the baby is mine.''

"What is it you think you *can* do, Nina?" He watched the resolve on her face weaken at his words and wondered why it gave him so little satisfaction. "Take my sister and her husband to court? What lawyer in his right mind would even take your case? You don't have any proof because there is no proof.''

"Oh, yes, there is.'' She stared at him with an intriguing mixture of defiance and fear. Doubt and absolute determination. But there wasn't a trace of insanity in her eyes.

Should he be relieved or terrified? Grant wondered. Aloud he said, "What proof do you have?"

"DNA."

Memories rushed through Grant's head. He'd once been faced with the prospect of taking a DNA test himself, and though it hadn't come to that, the experience was still one he didn't care to dwell on. He said slowly, "You're asking my sister to subject herself and her family to DNA testing because of your accusation? Why should she do that? The burden of proof is on you."

Nina's gaze narrowed on him, as if she had somehow guessed the true nature of his hesitancy. "Is there some reason why your sister would be afraid of a DNA test?"

"Of course not."

"Then what has she got to lose? If the tests prove the baby is hers, I'll go away and you'll never hear from me again. I won't make any trouble for your family. You have my word on that."

"After tonight, I don't know that you're in any position to bargain that strongly," Grant countered.

"My sister could get an injunction against you. You wouldn't be allowed anywhere near her or her baby. If you did, you'd be sent back to jail."

Nina flinched. "I'm aware of that. But I also know people like you don't like adverse publicity. I'll take my story to the press if I have to. I'll make somebody listen to me, and then we'll see what happens. I wonder how well your sister will hold up under that kind of scrutiny?"

Whether she knew it or not, Nina had hit a nerve, and Grant took a moment to consider all his options. From what he remembered, DNA tests could be performed using a swab from inside the baby's mouth. It was a painless procedure for the child, and if it would put an end to Nina and her accusations, maybe the unpleasantness would be worth it.

Because after hearing her tonight, after seeing her, Grant knew she wouldn't let the matter drop. Somehow she had convinced herself that John David was her baby, and Grant had no doubt whatsoever that she would move heaven and earth to prove it.

In the meantime, the enormous strain his sister would be put under would threaten her health, and the inevitable publicity could damage the negotiations with Ventura. If the merger didn't go through, Chambers Petroleum could be in deep trouble. Grant had no intention of letting his sister's health or the imminent merger suffer.

"I'll have to talk to my sister before I can promise you anything," he said. "But if she agrees to the tests, I have a stipulation of my own."

Nina frowned. "What kind of stipulation?"

"We probably won't know the results of the tests for at least a couple of weeks. While we're waiting,

I don't want you talking to the police, to the press or even to an attorney. Don't speak to anyone about this. No more accusations, Nina. No more visits to my sister or her baby. Agreed?''

He could see the protest rising inside her, and then a cooler head seemed to prevail. She chewed her bottom lip for a moment, considering his demands. "We all go in at the same time for the tests," she said. "And the lab has to be one of both our choosing."

He shrugged. "Agreed."

"Agreed," she echoed solemnly, and held out her hand. Grant took it, letting his hand close over her fingers, feeling the warmth of her skin and suddenly remembering what it had been like to hold her in his arms. To kiss her.

In spite of her outrageous claims, he still found Nina Fairchild very attractive. Even knowing what a dangerous woman she truly was, he still found her alluring.

As if reading his mind, Nina removed her hand from his. "How soon will I hear from you?"

"Tomorrow," he promised. "The sooner we get this over with, the sooner we can all get on with our lives."

NINA WATCHED HIM drive away. Her legs trembled so badly she could hardly stand, but she wanted to make sure he was really gone. That he wasn't out there hiding somewhere, ready to do her in the moment she drifted off to sleep.

Now you really do sound crazy, she thought. But was it crazy to be afraid of the Chamberses and the Baldwins? They had money, power, friends in high places. Nina had no doubt they could simply make her disappear if they wanted to. Make her life a living nightmare if they chose to. Crazy would be to let down her guard, to trust any of them, including— or maybe even especially—Grant Chambers.

An uneasiness slipped over her as she watched the taillights of his car disappear around a corner. He'd seemed so wary when she'd first mentioned the DNA testing, but then he'd changed his mind. She couldn't help wondering why. Was it because he believed the tests would confirm that Vanessa had given birth to the baby, or because he intended to make certain the tests would provide those results?

Nina glanced at her watch. It was almost midnight. Grant promised she would hear from him tomorrow. That gave her only a few hours to do her homework.

But at least she had something concrete with which to occupy her time. Action she could take. For the first time in months, Nina's heart lifted. No longer would the police be in sole charge of the investigation. No longer would her baby's fate rest in the hands of strangers.

By morning she would have all the information on DNA testing that the Internet could yield. She would have lists of experts, doctors, and laboratories where the tests could be performed. When Grant Chambers called her, Nina would be ready for him.

And if he didn't call her back, he and the rest of his family were in for the fight of their lives.

Chapter Seven

Clayton was already in with J.D. the next morning when Grant entered the room. Even though Grant had been in his father's spacious office more times than he could count, the room still awed him a little, just as it had when he was a kid.

The space hadn't changed much over the years. The huge ironwood desk—handed down from when Grant's grandfather, Harlan Chambers, had been in charge—was still planted firmly in front of a row of floor-to-ceiling windows. The Remington bronzes still graced lighted pedestals, and the cornerstone of the office—the massive, well-stocked bar—still remained hidden behind a set of louvered double doors.

The man himself hadn't changed much, either. J. D. Chambers sat ramrod-straight in a high-backed leather chair that had always reminded Grant of a throne. His father's hair was a little grayer, maybe. His paunch a little more pronounced, but the firm set of his mouth and jaw and the hard glitter in his eyes were very much the same.

Clayton Baldwin, seated across from the desk, was a younger, thinner version of J. D. Chambers. Although his hair was blond where J.D.'s was dark, his eyes blue instead of gray, Clayton's expression was just as fierce, his gaze just as cold as the older man's.

And they both knew how to twist the knife in an enemy's back, Grant thought.

"I know what happened at the police station last night," J.D. said. "So just cut to the chase. How much does she want?"

Grant remained standing. "It's not quite as simple as that. I don't think she's after money."

J.D. sat back in his chair and glared at his son. "What the hell does she want, then?"

"She wants John David."

Clayton swore viciously. "She's insane. She has to be."

"I don't think so," Grant told him. "I think she's convinced herself the baby is hers."

"You believe that?" J.D. snorted. "It's as plain as the nose on your face what that woman is up to. She's trying to extort money from us." He wagged a finger in Grant's direction. "I will agree with you on one thing. She's not insane. I suspect she's very, very clever."

Clayton jumped to his feet and paced the office. "How the hell does she think she can get away with this? No one's going to believe her."

"Don't be too sure of that," J.D. said ominously. "By the time the press get through with her, guess who'll come out looking like the villain here? Chambers Petroleum, that's who. The merger with Ventura will be history."

Grant knew everything his father said was probably true. All except for Nina's plan to extort money from them. She wasn't after cash. She was fully convinced that her baby had been stolen by another woman—his sister. And that conviction worried Grant more than any extortion scheme could have.

"She can't get away with this," Clayton said darkly, spinning to face Grant. "*I'll* go see her this time, and believe me, when I'm finished with her, she'll wish she'd never heard of any of us."

"I wouldn't do that if I were you." An irrational anger surged through Grant, but he couldn't help it. Clayton was a pompous jerk who would think nothing of trying to intimidate Nina, or even threaten her, into backing down. And that would only make things worse.

Clayton's icy blue eyes narrowed on Grant. "Since when have you become this woman's defender? Is something more going on here that we don't know about?"

Grant turned back to his father, not bothering to respond. "I can tell you right now, threats aren't going to work with Nina. They'll only make her more determined. Let me handle her," he said. "I think I know a way to end this without anyone getting hurt."

"You had a chance to end it last night, and you didn't. Or *couldn't*," Clayton added sarcastically. "This concerns my family. My wife and my son. I'm the one who should be dealing with Nina Fairchild."

J.D. seemed to ponder the argument for a moment, then said, "Let me talk to Grant alone."

Clayton started to retort, then obviously thought better of it. With another killing look at Grant, he turned on his heel and exited the office.

J.D. tilted back his chair even farther and folded his arms across his middle. "I take it you've got something in mind?"

Grant hesitated. "Not exactly. But I've spent some time with Nina. I know what won't work with her."

His father considered this for a moment. "All right. I'll leave it up to you to handle her. But I want this situation taken care of with minimal damage to the family and to this company."

"So do I," Grant said. He would also like to make sure Nina wasn't caused any more pain than she'd already been through, but he didn't know if that would be possible. "I need Clayton to stay out of it."

J.D. nodded. "I'll take care of Clayton. Even if this does involve his wife and son, I don't trust him to handle a situation this delicate. He's too much of a hothead."

Grant's brows rose in surprise. "You trusted him enough to make him your vice president."

"Only because you weren't here."

And whose fault is that? Grant thought. *Who sent me to Venezuela for four years?*

"Clayton has a certain killer instinct that can be useful in a cutthroat business like this. You've always been a little too much like your grandfather to suit me," J.D. said bluntly. "The days of sealing deals with a handshake and a shot of whiskey are over, Grant. All that ended when the petroleum industry here in Houston went bust back in the eighties. Now it's dog-eat-dog, and I'll be honest with you. I've never been sure in my own mind that you had the stomach for what it takes to survive in the business these days."

The revelation didn't faze Grant. He and his father had never seen eye to eye on much of anything, least of all Chambers Petroleum. Grant's grandfather had

founded the company back in the thirties after dis-
covering oil on a small patch of farmland, and he'd
run the company for years with honor and integrity,
keeping it small and local, making deals with nothing
more than his word, never straying from the princi-
ples he held dear.

But when Grant's father took over the reins, he'd
had a different vision for the company, one that had
expanded and diversified Chambers Petroleum into
one of the largest independent oil companies in
Texas. And in so doing, he'd pretty much forsaken
the values Harlan had tried to instill in both his son
and grandson.

Grant wondered what his grandfather would say if
he could see the company now, if he could hear all
the wheeling and dealing that went on behind closed
doors.

"I haven't decided on my replacement when I retire," J.D. continued, as if he had read Grant's
thoughts. "But if you can handle this situation to my
satisfaction, I don't mind saying it'll go a long way
in your favor."

Grant stared at his father for a long moment, not
surprised but yet somehow disappointed that J.D.
would stoop to this level. "Am I supposed to look
at this as some kind of test?"

J.D. shrugged. "Look at it any way you like. Just
make the problem go away."

OUTSIDE IN THE HALLWAY, Clayton waited for him.
When Grant strode by, Clayton started to grab his
arm, then wisely thought better of it.

"What the hell are you planning to do?" he demanded, following Grant into his office.

Grant sat down behind his desk and leafed through his phone messages. "I'll take care of it. There's nothing for you to worry about."

"Damn you." Clayton planted his hands on Grant's desk and leaned toward him. "This is my wife and child we're talking about. I have a right to know what you're planning."

Grant smiled, knowing exactly how to infuriate his brother-in-law. "You're just going to have to trust me, Clayton, the way I trusted you four years ago. Of course, the next thing I knew, I was in Venezuela."

"That wasn't my doing. Your father made that decision."

Grant gave a short laugh. "With no input from you, I'll bet."

"You're up to something," Clayton accused. "You're trying to use this situation to your advantage."

"I'm trying to save my sister a lot of stress. I'm trying to save this company a lot of bad publicity. If that's using the situation to my advantage, then so be it."

Clayton's eyes narrowed as he glared at Grant. "I'm warning you. Don't try anything behind my back. I won't stand for it. I've got as much at stake in this company as you do. More so."

"How do you figure that?"

Clayton straightened and sneered down at him. "I'm family now. I'm married to J.D.'s little princess. And I gave him a *real* grandson."

Heat exploded inside Grant. He pushed his chair back and stood. "Get out of my face, Clayton. And get the hell out of my office."

Clayton lifted his hands in acquiescence. "All right, I'll go. For now. But just so you know, I'll be watching you. I don't want this situation turning into the same fiasco we had on our hands four years ago. I'm sure you don't, either."

When Clayton left his office, Grant strode across the room and slammed the door, rattling the framed photographs and certificates on his office walls. Although he hadn't been able to prove it, and still couldn't, Grant was sure Clayton had been behind his exile to South America. Grant wouldn't put it past his brother-in-law to have orchestrated the whole sordid mess, jeopardizing the company and an important deal just to make Grant look bad in his father's eyes.

Grant sat down in his chair and spun to face the windows, staring with a brooding frown at the crisp blue sky, marred only by the razor-thin trail of a jet. Clayton had accused him of trying to use the situation with Nina to his advantage, but if anyone was trying to make inroads, it was Clayton. Grant didn't trust him for a minute, and he knew his grandfather would be turning over in his grave at the prospect of his company being placed in the hands of someone so unscrupulous. Grant's father was one thing, but an outsider—

The pencil in Grant's hand snapped in two. Four years ago, Clayton Baldwin had outmaneuvered him. It was as simple as that. Grant had made the mistake of badly underestimating his adversary, but he would not make that same mistake twice.

He had a sudden, unexpected image of Nina Fairchild. Was he underestimating her, as well? Was she what she seemed—what he wanted her to be, he realized—or someone out for what she could get? Someone with a cold, devious plan?

Grant closed his eyes, resting his head against the back of his chair. Four years ago, another woman had been his downfall. Even more was at stake now. Not only his future, but whatever integrity remained of his grandfather's company.

"I don't like what your father has done to my company," his grandfather had told Grant, just a few weeks before the old man had died. Before Grant's whole world had come crashing down. "I don't approve of the way he does business, how he treats people. I'm counting on you to put things right."

A heavy burden, some might say, to put on the shoulders of a twelve-year-old, but a responsibility nonetheless Grant had taken seriously. He still took it seriously, although if he was honest with himself, he'd have to admit that what had once been a desire to please his grandfather had turned into a driving ambition of his own. Maybe even an obsession since Clayton Baldwin had come on board.

But regardless of his motivation, Grant had every intention of carrying out his grandfather's dying request.

He just wished Nina Fairchild had not become the obstacle standing in his way.

VANESSA, WEARING a blue silk robe and pajamas, lay on the chaise in her sitting room, flipping through a magazine when Grant walked in. She looked alarmingly pale and fragile this morning, and he felt immediately guilty for having been so concerned about the company and how all this would affect his father's decision. His sister was the one who had the most to lose. She was the one who had to be protected.

"I just looked in on John David," he told her. "I was surprised to see Alice Becker in there with him. Don't tell me you haven't fired her yet."

Vanessa closed the magazine and set it aside. "It's just temporary, until I can find someone else."

"The woman was drunk last night, Vanessa. How can you trust her with John David?"

Vanessa looked upset by his criticism. "It's not like I have a choice or anything. Dr. Sorensen has ordered me to bed for the rest of the week. There's no way I can take care of John David on my own. Besides, she promised she wouldn't drink anymore, and she's agreed not to leave the house with the baby. Mrs. Ellison will take him to the park every day," she said, referring to her housekeeper. "It's all under control. There's no need to worry."

Grant wasn't exactly convinced, but there wasn't a lot he could do about it. He pulled up a chair beside her chaise and sat down. "I didn't come here to talk about Alice Becker, anyway. I want to talk to you about Nina Fairchild."

When Vanessa remained silent, Grant added, "The woman who was in John David's nursery last night? The woman from the park yesterday?"

Vanessa winced. "Why didn't you tell me about that, Grant? I had a right to know."

He shrugged. "I didn't think it was important. I certainly didn't think she'd show up here last night."

He'd have thought it impossible, but Vanessa grew even paler. "Why is she doing this to me? Is she crazy? Is that why she's making these terrible accusations?"

Grant hesitated, unwilling to upset his sister further. But there were certain things that had to be discussed, decisions to be made, and Vanessa was the only one who could make them. "I don't think she's crazy. And I don't think any of this is personal. She's convinced herself that John David is her son."

"But why? That's what I don't understand. Why *my* son?"

"Because she thinks you stole *her* son. She thinks you masqueraded as a woman named Karen Smith in order to get close to her while she was pregnant. She thinks you came to the hospital the night her baby was born and took him."

"But this is insane!" Vanessa exploded. "She has to be out of her mind!"

The sudden color in her face alarmed Grant as much as her pallor had. "Calm down," he said quickly. "Don't get yourself all worked up about this. We can handle Nina Fairchild."

"How?"

"By proving to her that John David is your son."

Vanessa's blue eyes flashed in outrage. "Why should I have to prove anything to her? John David is *my* baby. I gave birth to him. There's no way she can take him away from me."

"Of course not," Grant agreed. "But she can put you through quite an ordeal."

"You don't think anyone's going to believe her, do you?"

"When you talk about something long enough and loud enough, someone is bound to believe you. She says that if she can find no legal recourse, she'll take her story to the press."

The angry color vanished from Vanessa's cheeks,

hollowing her face unattractively. "Oh, my God," she said. "Clayton would be furious. And Daddy—" She reached out and clutched Grant's arm. "This could jeopardize the Ventura merger, couldn't it? And if that happens, Chambers Petroleum could be in real trouble. Grant—"

He took her icy fingers in his. "I'm not nearly as pessimistic as the others. I don't think Nina Fairchild can do anything to hurt Chambers Petroleum or the Ventura merger. Right now, I'm more concerned about you."

Vanessa sat back against the chaise, biting her lip. "I know Grandfather always planned for you to take over the company, but it's my heritage, too." Her voice held an edge of bitterness that surprised Grant. "He and Daddy never wanted me to have anything to do with the business. They didn't think it was any place for a woman. I suspect you've always felt the same way," she said, looking betrayed.

"Not at all," Grant said. "If I've been reluctant to include you in the business, it's had nothing to do with your gender and everything to do with your health. I didn't want you under that kind of strain."

Vanessa's smile was wan. "Always the protective big brother, aren't you? Always there when I need you. So how are you going to slay this dragon for me, Grant?"

Grant remembered when Vanessa was ten years old and had had a serious bout with her heart. The doctors hadn't thought she would make it, and Grant had sat by her hospital bed for hours at a time, reading to her and telling her all about school, willing her to get better. And she had. When she'd opened her eyes and smiled at him, Grant had thought that he would do anything to keep his little sister safe. In spite of her faults, he still felt that way.

"I know it isn't up to you to prove or disprove anything Nina says, but it might be the easiest way to end all this. The quietest way."

A brief frown flitted across Vanessa's brow. "What have you got in mind?"

"DNA testing."

Her eyes widened in alarm. Her face turned even whiter as her breathing became labored. She started to tremble all over. "No! *No.*"

"Vanessa, calm down," Grant instructed. "Concentrate on your breathing. Where are your pills?"

She pointed to a table at the end of the chaise. Grant hurried over and found the medicine bottle, extracted a tiny white pill and filled a glass from the pitcher of fresh water. He handed the pill to her, and with a shaking hand, she put it in her mouth. Grant guided the glass to her lips, and she gulped water.

After a few moments, her trembling stopped and her breathing became even. She still looked far too white to suit Grant, but he wasn't unduly panicked. They'd been through this before.

"Should I call Dr. Sorensen?" he asked.

Vanessa shook her head. After a bit, she said weakly, "I'll be fine. I-it was just such a shock to hear you suggest such a thing."

"It's quite painless, if that's what concerns you," he said cautiously. "They swab the baby's mouth—"

"Please stop." One hand rested on her heart. She closed her eyes briefly. "There can be no DNA testing. No blood tests or anything like that. I won't stand for it."

An uneasiness crept over Grant. "Why not? It would prove once and for all that John David is your baby."

"I don't have to prove it," she whispered. "He *is* mine. Why should I subject my son and my husband to those tests because of that woman's outrageous claims?"

"The idea is to shut her up."

Vanessa flinched. "You'll just have to find another way."

"Do you mind telling me why?" Grant asked, his uneasiness deepening.

Vanessa's eyes flashed with sudden fire. "I just told you why."

"Yes, you did. But it's me you're talking to. I know you, Vanessa. I can always tell when you're hiding something. And I have to tell you, the possibilities are scaring the hell out of me right now."

She let out a long, shaky breath, drawing her legs up and wrapping her arms around her knees. She remained silent for a long moment, then she said, "You'll have to promise me nothing I say will leave this room."

Grant frowned. "I don't know if I can do that."

She glanced at him sharply. "It's not what you think. It's nothing that will compromise your sense of justice," she said almost angrily.

"All right," he agreed. "Tell me why you're so afraid of a DNA test."

She drew another long breath, averting her gaze. "Because Clayton isn't John David's father."

Grant sat stunned for a moment, unsure he'd heard her correctly. He leaned toward her. "Clayton isn't John David's father?"

A tear rolled down Vanessa's pale cheek. She shook her head.

Grant took another moment to digest the information. "Then who…?"

She reached for a tissue and dabbed at her eyes. "It doesn't matter. It was a terrible mistake. It happened when Clayton was out of the country so much, and I was lonely. An old friend called me up and asked me to dinner one night. I knew he'd always been attracted to me, and I think he sensed I was vulnerable that night. We had a few drinks, and…one thing led to another."

Grant hesitated. "How can I put this delicately?" he said, almost to himself. "How do you know Clayton isn't the father? I mean, the timing had to have been pretty close, or else he would have been suspicious."

A blush touched Vanessa's cheeks. "Trust me, I know." She squeezed her eyes shut. "Oh, God, if Clayton ever found out, I don't know what he'd do."

"He wouldn't lay a finger on you," Grant said grimly. "He wouldn't dare."

"I don't mean that." Vanessa wiped more tears. "Clayton would never hurt me. I know you've never liked him, Grant, but he's a good man. He loves me and John David. This would kill him, and Daddy—" She broke off, shuddering. "What would this do to him? He still thinks of me as his little princess."

The situation was ironic, Grant had to admit, and if he were a lesser man, he might even find it a little satisfying. He'd always been the black sheep of the family, the one who'd always garnered their father's disapproval. But most—if not all—of Grant's transgressions paled in comparison to this.

"You're worrying for nothing," he told her. "Clayton's paternity isn't in question here. What we're trying to do is convince Nina that you're John David's mother. Clayton wouldn't even have to be involved in the tests."

Vanessa looked up at him. "Are you sure of that?"

He hesitated. "No, but it stands to reason."

She shook her head. "That's not good enough. They might start looking at blood types, who knows what else. I know if I agreed to this, Clayton would somehow find out. I can't do it, Grant. I can't take that chance. You're going to have to find another way to stop that woman."

His sister grew agitated again, and Grant rushed to calm her. "Okay. Okay. Don't worry. I'll handle it. Just promise me you won't let yourself get all worked up about this."

She bit her lip and nodded. "All right, but you have to promise me you'll never reveal anything I've told you today."

"I won't," he vowed, standing to leave. But even as he promised, he remembered Clayton's taunt. *I have as much at stake in this company as you do. More so. I married his little princess. I gave him a real* grandson.

The thought occurred to Grant that he'd just been given the ammunition he needed to neutralize his adversary's power in Chambers Petroleum, but he couldn't use it.

Without knowing it, Clayton had just won another round.

IT TOOK NINA several minutes to answer her door. When she finally drew it back, Grant stared at her for a long moment, realizing that here was yet another side of this woman. She resembled neither the waiflike creature from the park nor the glamorous socialite from last evening. Instead, dressed in black corduroy slacks and a silver turtleneck, she appeared today to be a competent, self-assured young woman with a purpose. Highlights glimmered in her short hair as she stood back to allow him to enter.

He followed her into the living room and waited until she'd seated herself on the teal sofa before sitting down beside her. The glass-topped coffee table in front of them contained stacks of papers, and the heading "DNA" on one of the top sheets caught his eye.

He picked it up. "What's this?"

Nina shrugged. "I've been doing my homework. I was up most of the night researching DNA testing on the Internet. As you can see, I found quite a bit of information."

He looked at her. "You've read all this?"

"Most of it. I wanted to be prepared."

"I'm impressed," he told her. "You obviously know your way around the Net."

"I should." She smiled, and her eyes crinkled at the corners in a way Grant found very attractive. He caught himself wishing she would smile more often, but then, after the story she'd told him last night, he guessed she hadn't had much reason to. "I design web pages for small businesses, as well as doing research for several writers."

He glanced around, not seeing a computer. "You work from here?"

She nodded. "I have a small office in the back.

Look, I don't mean to sound rude, but I am anxious to find out what your sister had to say about the tests. Did she agree?''

Although she appeared calm and self-assured on the surface, Grant could see the telltale evidence of her nerves in the way she clasped her hands together. In the way her bottom lip trembled slightly before she bit it.

"I'm afraid the DNA tests are out of the question,'' he told her.

"Why?"

"My sister doesn't want to subject her family to the procedure.''

"But don't you see?" Nina cried, her expression more tragic than triumphant. "That means she has something to hide.''

"It means nothing,'' Grant said almost angrily. Though why he was suddenly mad at Nina he wasn't quite sure. "Vanessa doesn't feel she should have to prove anything to you. John David is her son.''

"But we agreed—"

"I agreed on the condition that I had to talk to my sister first. I did that, and now the test is no longer an option.'' When Nina would have protested again, he said, "But that doesn't mean this is over.''

"No, it doesn't,'' she agreed. Pausing, she gazed at him in earnest. "We could do the test without her permission. You could get the baby's DNA sample.''

He frowned. "You're asking me to go behind my sister's back? Betray her? I can't do that, Nina. Vanessa was very adamant about her wishes.''

"Then I don't see that we have anything else to talk about,'' Nina said.

"I can still prove to you that my sister gave birth to John David."

Nina looked at him doubtfully. "How?"

"By having you come with me. There's someone I'd like you to talk to."

"Who?"

Grant took her hand and was pleasantly surprised when she didn't try to withdraw it. "Just come with me. I promise I'm not up to any tricks."

Her hand trembled inside his. "Why should I trust you?"

Grant decided to lay all his cards on the table. "Because at the moment, what else are you going to do? Who else is going to help you?"

"*Help* me?" She did withdraw her hand then. Anger flashed in her eyes. "Is that what you're trying to do?"

"Won't it help you to know the truth? Isn't that what you want?"

Her gaze didn't waver from his. "I already know the truth. But I'll come with you for one simple reason. While you're trying to convince me that John David isn't my son, I just might be able to prove to you that he is."

Chapter Eight

They were silent in the car. Nina sat staring out the window, wondering if she'd made the right decision. Once they'd gotten on the freeway and were heading toward downtown, she'd asked Grant again where he was taking her, but all he would say was that she'd find out soon enough and not to worry, he wasn't trying to trick her.

But how could she believe him? How could she trust him when she knew he and his family would like nothing more than to find a way to send her packing?

She slanted him a glance, studying his profile for a moment as he watched the road. He was a very attractive man. She couldn't deny that. From the first moment she'd seen him in the park, his dark good looks and charisma had affected her in a way that was more than a little disturbing. He was her enemy, the brother of the woman who had stolen her baby, and yet when he'd kissed her last night, a tiny part of her had wanted to respond.

Nina remembered the feel of his lips on hers now and shivered, still watching him. If he kissed her again, would she succumb to the temptation? Would she kiss him back?

As if sensing her scrutiny, Grant turned suddenly, and for a split second, his gaze held hers. His eyes were impossibly dark and deep, fathomless in a way that made Nina wonder what he was thinking, and made her tremble at the possibilities. He had a way of looking at a woman—at her—as if he knew her every hidden desire. As if he knew things about her she didn't even know about herself.

"We're almost there." His voice sent a thrill of awareness through her. If she had been frightened by him before, she was absolutely terrified of him now. He had even more power than she'd originally thought. A dangerous kind of power that money had little to do with.

Tearing her gaze from his profile, she realized they were nearing the medical center. The huge hospital complexes and research centers rose in front of them, and Nina stared out her window, locating St. Mary's towering white facade as Grant exited the freeway and wove his way through the heavy lanes of traffic on Fannin Boulevard.

A few blocks over, on a narrow, tree-lined street, he pulled into a parking lot beside a building with white columns. The structure looked more like a private estate or one of the nearby art museums than a hospital, which a discreet sign near the entrance proclaimed it to be. As she stared at the building, a feeling of déjà vu came over Nina even though she knew she'd never been here before.

"What is this place?" she asked, as they got out of the car and crossed the parking lot to the building.

"This is the hospital where Vanessa had her baby."

Nina stopped at the bottom of the stone steps that led to the entrance. She glanced up at the impressive structure and suddenly realized why it seemed so familiar to her. Vanessa had been standing in front of this building in the picture Nina had seen last night.

"It's actually more of a residential hospital," Grant explained. "It's run by Dr. Ethan Carter and Dr. Thomas Hillcroft, both of whom are renowned ob-gyns. They established this facility for women who need around-the-clock medical care during their pregnancies."

"Such as Vanessa's heart problem?"

He gave her a sharp glance. "How did you know about that?"

"I was there last night when she collapsed, remember? I heard what you said to her and saw how frightened you both were."

Grant's gaze deepened. "Then you must understand why a speedy resolution to this matter is so important."

"It's important to me, too," Nina said quietly. She glanced back up at the hospital. "How long was she here?"

"For most of her pregnancy. She's arranged for us to speak with her doctor. He's expecting us." And with that, Grant took Nina's elbow and ushered her up the stairs.

Beneath the thin fleece jacket she wore, Nina could feel the slight pressure of his fingers, and she wondered why she didn't pull away. Why she didn't make it clear to him that she didn't need his help in any way.

Maybe because after so many months of feeling so alone, it was nice to have human contact, even if it was from a man she didn't trust.

The lobby of the hospital was as impressive as the exterior. Oriental rugs dotted green marble floors, and oil paintings lined pastel walls, but a faint antiseptic smell lingered in the air, giving away the true nature of the building. A receptionist, young and attractively groomed, sat behind a glass-topped desk and smiled warmly as they approached her.

Grant told her who they were, and she confirmed their appointment with a Dr. Ronald Mapleton. Five minutes later, another young woman, every bit as attractive as the first, appeared in the lobby to usher them back to Dr. Mapleton's office.

When the woman announced them at his office doorway, Dr. Mapleton looked up from the file he'd been studying, and an expression Nina couldn't quite define flashed over his features. He covered it with a tight smile and rose to greet them. But that first impression of a man none too happy to see them stayed with Nina. She couldn't help wondering what he was thinking beneath his benign expression.

The two men shook hands, and Dr. Mapleton, short, stocky and balding, reclaimed his seat and folded his arms on his desk. His hands drew Nina's gaze, and she had the unkind thought that his short, rather pudgy fingers didn't look as if they belonged to a doctor.

He gazed at his visitors over a pair of bifocals perched on the bridge of his nose. "How is it I can help you?"

"You spoke with my sister this morning," Grant said.

Dr. Mapleton nodded. "Yes. She told me about the unfortunate situation which has recently unfolded." A tiny pulse beat at the man's temple, and Nina watched it, almost mesmerized. Was it her imagination, or was Dr. Mapleton as nervous as she was?

Grant said, "Then you understand why she would like for you to show Mrs. Fairchild her medical records?"

"I know that's her wish, but I'm afraid I can't do that." Dr. Mapleton's glance darted to Nina, then back to Grant. "It's against hospital policy. I explained all that to Vanessa."

"Then we came here for nothing." Nina glanced at Grant. "This doesn't prove anything."

He started to respond, but Dr. Mapleton interrupted him. "On the contrary," he said. "Vanessa told me about your claim, and while I'm not at liberty to show you her records or to discuss her medical history in depth, I can assure you she was a patient of mine. She gave birth to a son in this hospital six months ago. Both mother and child were perfectly healthy when I dismissed them a few days later."

"You see?" Grant said softly.

The satisfaction in his tone angered Nina. If he thought convincing her was going to be that easy, he was sadly mistaken. "Can you tell me what time of day John David was born?" she asked Dr. Mapleton.

"It was late, around midnight, as I recall. Normally a patient with Vanessa's potential complications would have been transferred to one of the larger facilities, usually Texas Women's Hospital, but her labor progressed so rapidly there wasn't time to move her. She gave birth here, but she was never in any danger. We have excellent resources, and our staff are highly trained for every contingency.''

''You were present at the birth?''

His brows rose at her question. ''Of course.''

''There must have been other medical personnel present, as well,'' she persisted. ''Nurses, an anesthesiologist. A neonatal specialist, perhaps, or even a cardiologist.''

He dodged the question with professional aplomb. ''I can assure you, everyone was present who needed to be.''

''Could you supply me with the names of those who witnessed the birth?'' Although she wasn't looking at Grant, she sensed him tense, and wondered why. Was he worried about what she would learn here? Had he thought she would accept the doctor's word without question?

Dr. Mapleton scowled at her. ''I'm afraid it's also against hospital policy to release the names of staff members. Unless, of course, an official police investigation is involved. Which I gather this is not.''

''No, it isn't,'' Grant agreed. ''And I think we've taken up enough of your time.''

He started to rise, but Nina said, ''It was your idea to come here, and now that we're here, I still have more questions.''

Grant looked as if he wanted to argue, but he turned instead to the doctor. ''If you could just spare us a few more minutes.''

Dr. Mapleton nodded as he gave Nina a disdainful look. ''What else do you want to know?''

She shrugged. ''You say you delivered Vanessa Baldwin's baby here in this hospital six months ago.

But without seeing the records, all I have is your word on that, isn't it?''

Dr. Mapleton's ruddy complexion grew even redder. He removed his glasses and glared at her. "You have no reason to doubt my word, young lady. If you care to take the time to check into my background, you'll find my credentials are impeccable." As evidenced by the myriad of framed diplomas on his wall, Nina thought.

Still, something about him bothered her. Maybe it was because he was telling her exactly what she didn't want to hear, but Nina didn't trust him. And she certainly wasn't convinced by his story. Doctors, just like everyone else, had a price. They could be bought, and Vanessa Baldwin certainly had the means to do it. She could have left this hospital at any time and donned her Karen Smith disguise, especially if she had never even been pregnant.

"I understand this is a residential hospital," Nina said.

"That's correct."

"Your patients remain here for weeks, sometimes months at a time while they're pregnant?"

"Again, that's correct." He seemed to relax a bit. He sat back in his chair and steepled his fingers beneath his chin.

"During that time, are the patients allowed to leave the facility? You know, to go for walks or drives, or maybe even have weekend visits with their families?"

He grew instantly wary. "Most of our patients require complete bed rest, as well as constant monitoring. That's why their doctors admit them here in the first place."

"I understand that. But it is conceivable that one of your patients could have left the hospital without anyone knowing it, isn't it?" Out of the corner of her eye, she saw Grant turn and stare at her. Nina kept her gaze focused on Dr. Mapleton.

The pulse at his temple became even more pronounced. "We're not running a prison. Our patients aren't locked in their rooms, if that's what you mean."

"That's exactly what I mean," Nina said, her gaze probing his features. If Vanessa had never been pregnant, then this man had obviously been a conspirator.

He sat forward in his chair, his eyes flashing in anger. "I've told you everything you need to know. I trust this will end the controversy. Even though Vanessa Baldwin is no longer my patient, I'm still concerned about her. I would hate to see her put under the kind of stress that could irreparably damage her health." He slipped his glasses back on. "Now, if you'll excuse me, I really must get back to my work."

This time Grant stood immediately, as if he was just as anxious as the doctor to get Nina out of there. "Thanks for your help, Dr. Mapleton."

"Certainly."

Grant and Nina said nothing as they left the office and retraced their steps down the hallway to the lobby. Nor did they speak once they were outside crossing the parking lot to Grant's car. But as Nina started to climb inside, he caught her arm and she turned to look up at him.

"Are you all right?" His dark eyes studied her face.

She shrugged. "I'm fine. Why wouldn't I be?"

A brief shadow crossed his features. "Surely now you realize the mistake you've made. John David is Vanessa's son, Nina."

"I only realize the lengths some people will go to to make me believe that." She removed her arm from his hand. "That man was lying. Couldn't you tell? He could hardly look either one of us in the eye, and he couldn't wait to get rid of us."

"That's ridiculous and you know it. Why would he lie?"

"Maybe your sister paid him to."

"Nina—"

She put up her hand to silence him. "I know what you're thinking. What you're all thinking. I'm either crazy or out to get my hands on your money, or both. But I don't care what you think. I'm more convinced than ever that your sister stole my baby. And Dr. Mapleton, for whatever reason, is helping her cover it up."

"Nina, listen to me." Grant took her shoulders with both hands and turned her to face him. When she would have pulled away, his grasp tightened. He stared down at her, his eyes dark and angry, deep with emotion. "You have to face reality here. John David isn't your son. The longer you keep pretending he is, the harder it's going to be for all of us. I don't want to hurt you. That's the last thing I want. But I can't let you hurt my sister, either. I can't let you threaten her health."

"Then what am I supposed to do?" Nina cried. "Forget about last night? Forget I saw my dead husband in that baby's face? I *can't* forget. It was almost as if I were looking at Garrett himself."

Grant's expression altered subtly. Some indefinable emotion flickered in his eyes. "You were in love with him, weren't you? In spite of the impending divorce, you loved him and you must really miss him."

Anger, hot and furious, shot through Nina. She jerked herself away from his grasp. "I know what you're trying to do. You're trying to make me doubt myself, but it won't work. I know that baby is mine. I *know* it."

Grant's gaze hardened. "Then I guess we're back where we started. You have no way of proving Vanessa's baby is yours, and I can't seem to convince you that he's not. So where do we go from here?"

"For starters, you can take me home," she said coldly. "I have a lot of work to do."

"Contacting the media? The police? What are you going to do, Nina? Who's going to buy your story? You'll only cause more grief for yourself and a lot of other people if you don't drop this."

"I don't want to hurt anyone." Her voice trembled in spite of herself. She touched her fingertips to her lips. "I just want my baby back."

Grant paused, his gaze never leaving hers. For a long, tense moment, he said nothing. Then finally he spoke. "Supposing I told you I know another way to prove, without a shadow of a doubt, that Vanessa's son isn't yours."

Nina frowned, brushing the hair back from her face. "How can you prove it that conclusively without a DNA test?"

"There is a way."

"How?" she demanded, her tone openly distrusting.

"By finding *your* son." Grant's gaze softened as

he stared down at her, and unexpectedly Nina felt the sting of tears behind her lids. "Will you let me help you do that?"

She couldn't hold his gaze. Glancing away, Nina struggled for composure.

"My family has money, clout, influence with the police department," he said. "We could put pressure on the detective in charge of your case to give it priority. We could hire the best private investigators in the business to track down this Karen Smith and make her tell us what she did with your son."

"You think I haven't already done that?" A cold breath of wind blew down the collar of Nina's jacket, and she shivered, wrapping her arms around her middle as she glared up at Grant. "I hired an investigator, I hounded the police night and day, I passed out hundreds of flyers all over Galveston and Houston. I did the interviews, talked to people at the hospital, wrote dozens of letters to the governor, senators, anyone I could think of who might be able to help. But nothing *did* help. Not until I saw Karen Smith in the park yesterday. Not until I realized who she was and why she'd disappeared off the face of the earth. She took my baby and went back to her real life."

"But what if she didn't?" Grant asked softly. "What if you're mistaken about my sister? What if there's a chance that your baby is still out there somewhere, and with my help, you could find him? Are you *that* sure, Nina? Are you willing to pass up this chance?"

Yes, she thought. *I am that sure.*

But how could she prove it? Who would believe her? Grant was right. His family did have money, clout, influence with the police—and they could use all that against her, keep her from ever finding out the truth. Without Grant's help, what chance did she have against them?

And if she was honest with herself, Nina had to admit a tiny part of herself, an irrational part perhaps, wanted to believe that Grant truly desired to help her. That he was a decent, honest man who would do the right thing, even if it meant hurting his own sister.

"You've been all alone in this." His gaze was intense, his voice a velvet coercion. "You've had to fight this battle all by yourself for way too long, but not anymore. Let me help you, Nina. Let me help you find your son."

IT WAS AFTER EIGHT that night when Grant finally dropped Nina off at her house. They'd been together for over five hours—time that had been intense, intimate and far too revealing. She wasn't sure when it had happened, but their relationship had subtly changed over the course of the evening. They had become…not friends, exactly, but what? Cautious allies? Wary confidants?

Nina couldn't explain the way she felt about Grant Chambers. The negative emotions were still there, of course. The fear and distrust. The knowledge that the wealth and power he possessed epitomized everything in a man she had come to loathe. But she also sensed in Grant traits she admired and respected. Honor and integrity, and yes, even the loyalty he felt toward his sister.

Loyalty that could very well lead to her downfall, Nina reminded herself as she got ready for bed. She brushed her teeth and washed her face, then studied her reflection in the bathroom mirror, thinking back over the evening she'd just spent with Grant.

After leaving Dr. Mapleton's office, they'd driven around for a bit while Nina, at Grant's coaxing, had told him in more detail about the time leading up to Dustin's birth and the agonizing months since his disappearance. She told him everything she knew of the police investigation, the leads they'd followed, the witnesses they'd interviewed and the conclusions they'd drawn about Karen Smith.

Grant listened with avid interest, interrupting her only to ask a brief question now and then. Nina found herself pouring everything out to him, not just the facts, but also her feelings and emotions, her heart and soul, and once finished, she sat back in her seat, drained but oddly at peace.

She thought the evening would end at that point, but Grant hadn't driven her home immediately. Instead he took her to dinner at Americas, a beautiful restaurant in the Galleria area with the most unusual artwork decor Nina had ever seen. He seemed to know the management, and they were given an intimate corner table on the upper level that made Nina wonder about the other women he had undoubtedly taken there.

They placed their orders, including a bottle of wine, and after the waiter departed, Grant folded his arms on the table and stared at her over the flickering candle. Rather than resuming their previous conversation, he told her about his four years in Venezuela, charming her with his descriptions of the country and the people, amusing her with anecdotes about the trials and tribulations of being in charge of an operation so remote, half the time the roads were impassable and the other half merely treacherous. Not to mention the bandits, he added. And to make his life even more interesting, no one on the crew or in the office spoke anything but Spanish.

By the time the evening drew to an end, Nina looked at Grant with new eyes, and she realized he hadn't always led the pampered life she'd assumed. It was true he was from a wealthy and powerful family, but he had worked hard and taken a lot of risks to get where he was in the world. He was not a man who would ever be content to rest on his family's laurels. Grant Chambers would want to leave his own mark.

So where did she fit into that ambition? Nina wondered as she climbed into bed. Why was he so anxious to help her find her son?

And more importantly, could she trust him? If he uncovered evidence that proved his sister had stolen Nina's baby, would he use the information to return her son to her, or would he bury it in order to protect his sister?

FIVE MINUTES after dropping Nina off at her house, Grant pulled into the covered parking area of his apartment complex off Memorial Drive. He wondered what she would say if she knew how close they lived to one another. Would she be comforted or disturbed by the proximity? Grant wanted to believe he'd made inroads against her distrust tonight, but he couldn't be sure of his success.

Letting himself into the apartment, he poured a drink and carried it into the bedroom, then stretched out on the bed, folding his hands behind his head as he listened to his messages. The first two were from his father and Clayton, demanding to know what was happening with Nina, and the third message was from Trent Fairchild. Grant sat up on the edge of the bed at the sound of his friend's voice.

"Hey, Grant, it's Trent. Sorry I missed you. Listen, I got a call today from your brother-in-law. He said you guys are having some trouble with Nina Sparrow. You probably know her as Nina Fairchild, but I still can't bring myself to call her that. Anyway, I didn't go into a lot of detail about her on the phone with Clayton, but I think you and I need to talk. That woman is bad news, buddy. Give me a call as soon as you get in."

Grant glanced at his watch. It was only a little after eight-thirty, still early enough to call Trent in San Antonio, but for some reason, Grant hesitated. Did he really want to know what his friend had to say about Nina?

Muttering an oath, he jerked up the phone and dialed Trent's number. The phone rang several times before the housekeeper finally answered.

"Fairchild Residence."

"Trent Fairchild, please. This is Grant Chambers."

"I'm sorry, Mr. Chambers, but Mr. Fairchild is out for the evening. He isn't expected back until much later. Would you like to speak with Mrs. Fairchild?"

Grant hesitated. What would Edwina have to say about her ex-daughter-in-law? Nina had given him the definite impression that she hadn't gotten along with any of the Fairchilds because they hadn't considered her good enough for Garrett. But was there another reason for the animosity?

He asked the woman to put Trent's mother on, and

while he waited, Grant recalled the last time he'd seen Edwina Fairchild, just before he'd left for Venezuela. He'd been in San Antonio on business, and she and Trent had asked him to dinner. Garrett had been there, too, and Grant's negative opinion of the younger Fairchild son had been borne out once again. He had thought Garrett shallow and self-absorbed, the pampered baby of the family whom Edwina had almost obsessively doted on. No wonder she hated Nina. Edwina would have hated any woman who competed with her for her son's affection.

And Nina, Grant thought, would have made a formidable adversary. What man could resist that intriguing mixture of strength and vulnerability, that quiet beauty?

"Grant? My goodness, is that really you?" Edwina's voice sounded years older than Grant remembered. Garrett's death had obviously taken a toll.

"Hello, Edwina. How are you?"

"As well as can be expected. I received your note after Garrett's death. Thank you for being so thoughtful."

"I'm sorry I couldn't be there for the funeral." An uncomfortable pause ensued. Finally Grant said, "In a way, Garrett is the reason I'm calling. Actually I wanted to talk to you about…his wife. Nina."

He heard the sharp intake of Edwina's breath, as if he'd caught her by surprise—and not pleasantly so. "She is not a person I wish to discuss. Garrett was divorcing her at the time of his death. And with good reason, I might add."

"May I ask what that reason was?"

Another pause. "Why do you want to know?"

"My family has recently had some contact with

her. I don't really want to go into the specifics over the phone, but I wondered if you could give me some information about her background. Where she came from. How she and Garrett met.''

"She stalked him.''

An eerie chill crept up Grant's spine. That was the exact term Nina had used to describe Karen Smith. *The police think she stalked me.* "Can you explain that?'' he asked Edwina.

"She and Garrett met by chance at one of the museums here in town. It was a harmless meeting, one Garrett would have forgotten about in no time, except that Nina wouldn't let him forget. When she found out who he was, that he came from money, she began to follow him around, calling him at all hours, showing up wherever he went. And Garrett—'' Edwina broke off, overcome with emotion. After a moment, she continued. "Garrett found the attention flattering. He decided he was in love with her.''

An odd way of putting it, Grant thought, but he said nothing.

"I knew nothing about this, of course, although Trent admitted later he suspected something was going on between them. He had her background thoroughly investigated, and he found something that distressed him. But before he could disclose the information, Garrett and Nina turned up married. She tricked him into believing she was something other than what she really was. She made Garrett think she was a woman who needed taking care of, and he was vulnerable to that sort of thing. At least for a while. Then he began to realize what kind of person she really was, and what a horrible mistake he'd made in marrying her."

"What exactly did Trent find out about her?" Grant asked, mentally bracing himself.

"I never knew for sure, only that it was bad. She was raised in an orphanage, you know. I think it had something to do with an adoption that never went through."

An adoption? It hit Grant with something of a shock how little he knew of Nina's past. After tonight he thought he'd learned a lot about her, but he certainly hadn't known she'd been raised in an orphanage. In some ways, that explained a lot about her.

To Edwina, he said, "I appreciate your help, but I won't take up any more of your time tonight. Would you mind telling Trent I called?"

"Of course. It was good to hear from you, Grant. I don't talk to many people these days." She sounded old and lonely, and Grant wanted to feel pity for her, but he couldn't help remembering what Nina had said, that neither Trent nor Edwina had wanted anything to do with Nina's baby. Edwina couldn't help growing old, but she didn't have to be lonely. She didn't have to wallow in her bitterness.

When he would have hung up, she stopped him. "Grant...one more thing." She paused. "Nina is a very clever and dangerous woman. I don't know what she's up to now, or what she may be trying to do to your family, but don't ever make the mistake of trusting that woman."

Chapter Nine

Two days later, Grant showed up unannounced at Nina's door. She hadn't heard from him since the night they'd had dinner, and was about to decide to take matters into her own hands. She'd promised him she wouldn't go to the media with her story until she'd given him a chance to pursue an investigation into Dustin's disappearance, but she was running out of patience. The longer she was away from her son, the harder it would be to make up for lost time.

The moment Grant walked into her living room, Nina knew something was wrong. There was a subtle distance in his eyes, a new wariness in his features, and when she asked him to sit, he remained standing, as if knowing how intimidating and imposing he was to her.

"I think we should take a drive down to Galveston today," he said. "I'd like to talk to the detective in charge of your case and see if anything new has turned up."

"Nothing has," she said. "I spoke with him this morning."

Grant gave her a sharp glance. "Did he call you or did you call him?"

Nina frowned. "What difference does it make? I stay in touch with him constantly."

"Yes," Grant said. "I'm sure you do. At any rate, I'd like to speak with him in person, and I think he'd be more willing to talk to me about the case if you were along. I'd also like to see where you lived down there, the hospital, your doctor's office, everything."

Nina's frown deepened. "Why?"

"Because I want to know exactly what happened. I want to reconstruct the night your baby was stolen right down to the most insignificant detail. You're the only one who can help me do that."

Nina turned away, her heart starting to pound in agitation. What was he really trying to do? After their dinner the other night, she wanted more than anything to trust him, but she couldn't. Not when the warmth had gone from his voice, and his eyes held more than a trace of suspicion.

"I can't be expected to take off at a moment's notice. I have work to do," she said.

Grant lifted a brow. "I assumed since you're self-employed you could set your own hours. Besides, you don't really have to work if you don't want to, do you? Didn't you get a settlement from the Fairchilds?"

Nina's uneasiness grew. "I told you before, I didn't want a settlement from Garrett. After he died, I was the beneficiary of a life-insurance policy he'd taken out, but it certainly wasn't enough to retire on. I used some of the money to hire a private investigator, but I've put most of it away for my son's education." Nina wondered why she felt compelled to explain herself to him, of all people.

Because someone has told him something about

me, she thought. *Because he's starting to believe the lies just as Garrett did.*

He and Trent Fairchild were friends. It didn't take a brain surgeon to figure out whom Grant had been talking to, and why his attitude toward her had changed. Nina didn't want to resent that change, but she couldn't help it. She didn't want to care what he believed about her, but she did.

"If you can't get away this afternoon, I can make the trip to Galveston alone," Grant said. "I can talk to Sergeant Farrell without you, but I assumed you'd want to be present."

His tone held a slight challenge, as if he was daring her not to go with him. Whatever romantic thoughts Nina might have been harboring about him since their dinner vanished.

He was still the enemy. Why had she ever allowed herself to believe otherwise? He had his own agenda, and Nina would be a fool to forget that fact. She'd be an even bigger fool to think that he would turn his back on his own sister for her.

And Nina was no fool. She was a woman determined to get her son back, even if that meant pretending she didn't recognize Grant's motives. Because like it or not, he was her only connection to her son right now. The closer she remained to Grant Chambers, the closer she could get to her baby.

AN HOUR LATER, they left the causeway bridge that connected Galveston Island to the mainland, and merged with traffic on Broadway, a street lined with palm trees and turn-of-the-century mansions.

Nina directed him to the apartment complex where she had rented a small furnished unit by the month when Dr. Bernard had transferred to Galveston. The apartments filled up fast in the summer, but Nina had been there in late spring, before school was out, and the complex had been almost deserted. She hadn't gotten to know any of the other tenants, all of whom had long since moved on.

The manager had no recollection of Nina, nor could she recall seeing anyone with dark hair and glasses lurking about the place—but that didn't mean there hadn't been, she said, eyeing Grant with open interest. They got all kinds of weirdos down here, she added, glancing at Nina.

They left the apartment complex and drove to the medical center, where Dr. Bernard's office was located and where the skeletal remains of the burned-out hospital had been cleared away to begin construction on a new facility.

Grant pulled the car to the curb, and Nina got out, staring at the workers busy with their jobs, but seeing in her mind the frantic movements of the hospital personnel on the night of the fire. Hearing the sound of sirens, the frightened screams of the patients. Remembering her terror, not for herself, but for Dustin. She had been so frightened that he might not be moved to safety in time, but she had never dreamed that the fire had been started because of him. Because someone wanted him for her own.

Grant got out of the car and came around to stand beside her. "This was a fairly small hospital," he said. "There couldn't have been that many patients at any given time. Why were they taken to Houston instead of one of the hospitals here in Galveston? The UT medical branch is just a few blocks away."

"St. Mary's in Houston owns this hospital," Nina

told him. "No one ever said for sure, but my guess is that they took as many of us to St. Mary's as they could for insurance purposes. Kept everything nice and neat that way."

"Did you ever consider suing?"

Nina turned to him in surprise. "No. As far as I know, no one connected to the hospital had anything to do with the fire or my baby's disappearance. What would a lawsuit accomplish? It wouldn't bring back my son."

Grant stared down at her for a long moment, as if he couldn't quite figure her out. Then he shrugged. "I guess you're right. Maybe we'd better get going. Sergeant Farrell is expecting us."

SERGEANT FARRELL GREETED Nina cordially, if a bit coolly. His attitude toward her had changed since the night she'd been taken to the police station in Houston and she'd called him to come to her rescue. He'd made it clear that night that she couldn't count on him again, and today his demeanor seemed to reinforce that sentiment. Nina wondered if Grant noticed the detective's reticence toward her.

After a few minutes of conversation, Grant asked to see the file on Dustin's disappearance. Sergeant Farrell hesitated for a moment, then plucked the thick folder out of a drawer and slid it across his desk to Grant.

"Nothing in there you can't see," Farrell said, as if explaining his action. If there had been anything sensitive in the file, Nina was sure he had removed it before they came.

Grant opened the folder and began perusing the documents. After a moment, he pulled a page from the report and studied it briefly. "It says here you were carried unconscious from the burning hospital by one of the firemen."

She nodded. "I was somehow knocked unconscious before I could get out of the building."

He glanced up. "Somehow?"

Nina shrugged. "I don't know what happened. I stayed inside to make sure my baby had been taken to safety. As I was leaving the nursery area, I thought I saw someone still in the building. I turned to call out, but then part of the ceiling collapsed and I was knocked unconscious, presumably by falling debris. If the fireman hadn't found me—" She broke off, shuddering, and saw Grant's gaze darken before he glanced back down at the report.

"It also says here that the doctor who treated you outside noticed that your hospital ID bracelet was missing." This time instead of looking at Nina, Grant trained his gaze on Sergeant Farrell. "Any idea how that happened?"

Before Farrell could answer, Nina said, "I've always thought whoever took Dustin removed my bracelet."

Farrell shrugged. "It's possible. It's also possible someone else removed it."

"Like who?" Nina asked.

His gaze met hers. "You tell me."

As his words sunk in, Nina stared at him with dawning horror. "You don't think *I* cut it off?"

"I didn't say that."

"But that's what you were implying," Nina said angrily. She stared at Farrell for a long moment, until he finally glanced away. "Why would I do such a thing?" she demanded.

He hesitated, then said, "Look, I don't necessarily think you did, okay? But I have to look at every possibility."

Dear God, Nina thought. Someone had gotten to Farrell, too. Someone had told him the same lies that had been told to Grant, and in the course of a few days, Nina had gone from victim to suspect. She felt as if a noose were being slowly tightened around her neck, and there was no one to cut her loose.

She took a deep breath, trying to settle the sick feeling growing in the pit of her stomach. "Could I get some water?"

Farrell nodded toward the door of his office. "Cooler's just down the hallway. Make a left."

Reluctantly Nina stood, torn between needing some air and not wanting to leave the two men alone to discuss her further. She glanced at Grant, but he was studying the file again and didn't seem to notice when she left.

The knots inside her stomach coiling even tighter, Nina turned and went in search of the water cooler.

"THERE'S ALWAYS BEEN something just a little odd about Nina," Farrell said reluctantly.

Grant was standing at the window, and he turned now to stare at the detective. "In what way?"

"Hard to say." Farrell scowled at the pile of paperwork on his desk. "Her reaction to her son's kidnapping, for one thing. She never really lost it, if you know what I mean. Never showed the kind of emotion you'd expect from something like that."

A spark of anger flared inside Grant. "Different people react to tragedy in different ways."

"True enough," Farrell agreed. "But I never saw

her shed so much as a single tear. She didn't show much emotion one way or another.''

Her stoicism was one of the traits Grant admired most about Nina. It was also one that intrigued the hell out of him. What would happen if she ever did lose control? Grant thought that, depending on the circumstances, he just might like to be around when that happened.

''Are you trying to tell me that Nina is a suspect in her baby's disappearance?'' he asked.

Farrell hesitated. ''Everyone who had any contact with her baby is a suspect. I don't know how much you know about Nina's background, but she has no family. No friends to speak of, either. She's a real loner. None of her neighbors in Houston even knew she was pregnant. Neither did her husband's family, for that matter. I find it a little strange that she never told anyone about her pregnancy. Why would she keep it a secret?''

''Are you sure she never told the Fairchilds about the baby?''

''They claim she didn't.'' Farrell paused again. ''I don't like to say this, but...there may be more going on here than you realize.''

''Such as?''

The detective met Grant's gaze. ''Like I said, Nina's reaction to her baby's disappearance has always bothered me. Lately I've begun to ask myself some pretty tough questions. Like, what if she never intended to keep the baby in the first place? What if she...did something to him, and then concocted this whole story just to cover her tracks?''

Grant stared at him in shock. ''You don't really believe that.''

Farrell shrugged. ''I know it sounds bizarre, but believe me, I've seen and heard it all.''

''But Nina gave birth in the hospital just a few hours before the baby disappeared,'' Grant argued. ''She wouldn't have had time to…do anything to him.'' He could hardly bring himself to put Farrell's ludicrous speculation into words. The notion of Nina being anything other than a loving mother was just too incongruous with what Grant had come to believe about her.

''Actually,'' Farrell said slowly, ''there's no proof of the baby's birth. The records were all destroyed in the fire, and Nina's obstetrician, a Dr. Bernard, didn't make it to the hospital until after Nina had the baby. He vouched for the fact that she was pregnant, but not that she gave birth that night. And he can't even corroborate her pregnancy now. I just found out that he's conveniently out of the country and won't be back for months.''

''What about the doctor who delivered the baby?'' Grant asked, more disturbed by the conversation than he wanted to admit.

''Nina said a resident named Wharton handled the delivery. The only Wharton on duty that night is now in rehab. He broke into a drug closet the night of the fire, and made off with some pretty heavy-duty medications. He was a suspect for a while, but he's been cleared of the arson charges. His license to practice medicine has been revoked, however, and he doesn't even remember the fire, let alone delivering a baby that night.''

''The nursing staff?'' Grant asked hesitantly, almost afraid to hear Farrell's answer. Wasn't this what he wanted? A way to discredit Nina's story? A way to stop her from destroying his family?

Why wasn't he happy, then?

"There is that," Farrell agreed. "One of the nurses remembers Nina. Her name is Ruthanne Keller. She was the floor nurse on the maternity ward the night of the fire."

"Is she the one who saw a dark-haired woman claiming to be Nina's sister near the delivery room?"

Farrell glanced at him in surprise. "How did you know about that?"

"Nina told me."

Farrell nodded. "Keller recanted that claim after the fire. Said she couldn't be sure the woman told her she was Nina's sister. She might have been there to see one of the other women in Labor and Delivery."

"You checked that out, I take it?"

"Two other women gave birth that night. Neither of them had a sister visiting."

"So that does corroborate Nina's story."

"To a certain point. But there is still the matter of the missing ID bracelet."

Grant glanced over his shoulder. Nina still hadn't returned, and he couldn't help feeling guilty for talking about her behind her back. "She said she thought someone was still in the hospital with her before she lost consciousness, possibly from being struck by fallen debris. But whoever took the baby could easily have knocked Nina unconscious and removed the bracelet, just like she said."

Farrell studied him for a moment. "Why would someone who had started a fire in order to steal a baby stick around long enough to knock the mother unconscious and cut off her ID bracelet? It doesn't make sense.''

''But you said you didn't think Nina had removed the bracelet.''

''No, I said I had to look at every possibility.'' Farrell sat back in his chair and ran his hand through his hair. ''I don't know what to think. There are just too many damn inconsistencies in this case.''

Grant walked over to the door and stared out the glass panel, looking for Nina. ''How long have you had these doubts about her?''

''All along, to a certain degree, but they escalated when she started all this business about your sister and Karen Smith being the same person. That's when I began to worry that maybe she'd gone off the deep end.''

''Why are you telling me all this?'' Grant turned to face the detective. It seemed to him that Farrell was being candid above and beyond the call of duty.

Farrell studied the floor for a moment, as if searching for the right answer. When he looked up, his gaze was shadowed. ''Look, in spite of what I've just told you, I like Nina. I think she's had a lot of tough breaks in her life, but I wouldn't be much of a cop if I didn't at least clue you in on my concerns. I'm worried about her. About what she might do. I don't want to see anybody get hurt. If you've got a way to defuse this situation before it gets out of hand, I think you'd better do it. Not just for Nina's sake, but for your sister's, as well.''

''SO WHAT DID YOU TWO talk about while I was gone?'' Nina asked. They were back in Grant's car, heading over to one of the local hospitals where

Ruthanne Keller was now employed. Nina had spoken with the nurse twice after Dustin's disappearance, and neither time had been a particularly successful interview. She wondered if Grant would have better luck with the nurse than she'd had. Somehow she thought he might. What woman wouldn't be willing to bare her soul to a man as attractive as Grant Chambers?

When he glanced in her direction, Nina suppressed a shiver. "Well? Are you going to answer me?"

He shrugged. "We talked about the case."

"Did you learn anything new?"

Grant paused. "Hard to say."

"Either you did or you didn't," Nina said impatiently. "Why the equivocation?"

"Look." He rubbed the back of his neck as he kept his eyes trained on the road. "I just want to keep an open mind while we gather all the information we can. I don't want to draw any conclusions, okay?"

That wasn't what she was asking him to do, but for some reason he seemed unwilling to give her a straight answer to her question. Nina wondered again what he and Farrell had discussed while she'd been out of the office, and whom Farrell might have spoken with before she and Grant arrived. She realized her thoughts were becoming more and more mistrustful all the time, but Nina couldn't help it. It was as if someone was working behind the scenes to discredit her, first with Grant and now with Sergeant Farrell. Someone who wanted to make sure Nina never learned the truth about her baby.

The obvious person was Vanessa, but Nina knew

that no one could plant suspicion like Trent Fairchild. Could he be involved in this in some way?

Nina started to ask Grant straight out if he had been in touch with Trent, but just then, he pulled the car into the parking garage of the hospital and they got out to go in search of Ruthanne Keller.

She was working a double shift and wouldn't be able to talk to them until after she got off at seven. If they cared to come back then, they could ask her anything they wanted, but her answers wouldn't be any different, she warned Nina.

"There's a little café called Antoinette's a couple of blocks over on Smith," she said, glancing at her watch. "I usually stop in there after work and have a bite to eat."

"We'll be there," Grant said. "But just one quick question before we go." He withdrew a photograph from his jacket pocket and laid it on the desk in front of Ruthanne. Nina saw that it was a picture of Vanessa, and her heart started to pound in alarm. "Does this look like the woman you saw the night of the fire? The one who may or may not have claimed to be Nina's sister?"

The nurse studied the photograph, then glanced up. "Like I told the police, that woman had dark hair. She didn't look anything like this person."

"You're absolutely sure?" Grant insisted. "Look closely."

"Look at the eyes," Nina said, and when Grant glanced at her, she returned his gaze almost defiantly.

Ruthanne shook her head. "I'm sorry, but this woman doesn't look at all familiar to me."

She started to turn away, but Nina said, "Wait." Extracting a black pen from her purse, she quickly darkened Vanessa's hair and sketched a pair of glasses on the face. The hasty marks were disconcerting at first, but the more Nina darkened the hair, the more Karen Smith's features started to come through.

Ruthanne stared down at the photograph with a kind of curious fascination. She watched Nina's pen strokes as if mesmerized.

Nina glanced up. "Now do you see a resemblance?"

Ruthanne picked up the photograph and studied it again. After a long moment, she said, "I'm not sure. This could be her, I guess."

"But if I were to show you almost any woman's picture that had been doctored in this manner, you might think the same thing. Isn't that right?" Grant pressed her.

Ruthanne never took her eyes off the picture. "There *is* something about her eyes," she murmured, almost to herself.

Nina's heart jumped in elation. "Then you do recognize her?"

"I still can't say for sure." Ruthanne glanced up. "I really do have to get back to work, but can I keep this picture? I'll bring it with me when I meet you later."

Grant nodded. "Sure." Then he turned to Nina, his expression unreadable. "Let's go."

"THAT ISN'T PROOF," he declared, as they drove away from the hospital. "You do realize that."

"It may not be proof, but it's a start." When he said nothing else, Nina folded her arms over her chest. "I know that isn't what you want to hear. I know you don't want to believe your sister is in-volved in this. You brought me down here to prove to me she isn't. But what if it doesn't turn out that way? What if we learn just the opposite? What will you do then?'' she challenged.

Grant shot her a quick glance. "I promised you I'd help you find your baby and I will."

"No matter what?"

"No matter what." He watched the road with grim determination. "I know how much you want to be-lieve John David is your baby, because that would mean your search is over and that your son is safe and sound. But as much as you believe John David *is* your son, I believe he isn't. If I'm to keep an open mind about this investigation, Nina, so must you."

"Is there any way I can see him again?" The question surprised her as much as it seemed to sur-prise him.

He pulled to the curb and parked, then turned to stare at her for a long moment. "I don't think that would be such a good idea. Vanessa would never agree to it."

"I know she wouldn't, but you could arrange it if you wanted to."

He searched her face. "Do you know what you're asking of me?"

"Yes." Nina gazed up at him. "I wouldn't ask if I didn't think my son's life was at stake. I don't want to hurt you or your family. In spite of what you may have heard about me, I'm not a bad person."

Again he hesitated. His gaze seemed to soften. "I never thought you were. I wouldn't be here if I did."

Tentatively Nina touched his sleeve. "Then you'll arrange for me to see the baby again?"

"I can't do that." He took her hand in his. "I hope you understand, but I can't go behind Vanessa's back like that. Not even for—" He broke off, leaving Nina to wonder what he might have been about to say.

"But what if I were to see him again and realize I was wrong about him? What if I realize what a terrible mistake I've made? Wouldn't it be worth going behind your sister's back to find that out?"

"But that's not why you want to see him again, is it?" His fingers caressed the back of her hand, and Nina felt a shiver of awareness race through her. "You're still thinking about the DNA test, aren't you?"

In the back of her mind, perhaps she had been thinking that if she could just be alone with the baby, if she could just get a sample of his DNA, she could prove once and for all he was her son.

"We could end all this so easily, Grant."

His expression hardened. "It wouldn't be easy for me."

"I know it wouldn't. But...I have to see him, Grant. Please."

"Nina—"

"I can't stand *not* seeing him, not holding him, not having him in my life." She drew a ragged breath. "You have no idea what this is like for me."

He leaned toward her, his eyes deep and dark, full of compassion and another emotion Nina couldn't quite read. "I know it's hard. It's difficult for everyone. That's why we're doing this. We're going to learn the truth about your son, Nina."

She stared into his eyes, her hand trembling inside his. "I wish I could believe that."

"You can."

"You're willing to ask questions, hire investigators, use your influence with the police, but you're not willing to do the one thing that could end this."

"I can't."

"Then I don't see that we have anything else to talk about." She withdrew her hand from his, feeling suddenly alone and bereft. "I don't even know why I came down here with you."

"Because you know in your heart it's the right thing to do."

"I only know that I'm dying inside," she whispered, fighting back tears. "Each and every day I'm away from my son."

"Then all the more reason why we should be here." His hand brushed against her hair, a touch so light Nina thought she might have imagined it. "All the more reason why we have to do everything in our power to find out the truth about your son."

Chapter Ten

They decided to have an early dinner while they waited for Ruthanne Keller's shift to end. Grant drove them to a restaurant near the pier with an incredible view of the gulf.

They took a seat near the windows, and instead of studying the menu, Nina found herself watching the graceful swoop of the seagulls as they searched the sand for food. Beyond the shoreline, the first of the fishing boats glided home for the night as the sun dipped lower into the sea, and the golden sparkle on the water slowly turned to silver.

The scene was one of profound serenity, and for the first time in a very long time, Nina slowly began to relax.

They said hardly anything after they'd placed their orders, but finally, when their salads had been removed and steaming bowls of seafood gumbo had been set before them, Grant began to question her, first about her work, and then, when she reluctantly started to open up to him, he wanted to know more about her background.

"I grew up in an orphanage in San Antonio," she said, taking a sip of her water. She returned the glass to the table, glancing up to find Grant watching her. She met his gaze steadily. "But I suspect you already know that."

To his credit, he didn't try to deny it. "Edwina told me."

"So you've been talking to the Fairchilds." Nina told herself she was foolish for feeling so betrayed, but she couldn't help it. "Did you call Edwina or did she call you?"

He hesitated for a moment. "Actually I tried to call Trent, but he wasn't in. He'd left a message on my machine, saying he wanted to talk."

"About me?"

Another hesitation. "Yes."

"When was this?" Nina asked, trying to tamp down an unreasonable spurt of anger.

"A couple of days ago."

That explained the change in Grant's attitude when he'd first shown up at her door this afternoon. Her guess had been right. The Fairchilds had gotten to him.

"What else did Edwina tell you?" she asked coolly.

"Not much." Grant picked up his wineglass, eyeing her over the rim. "Only that you had been raised in an orphanage, and that something had gone wrong with an adoption. What happened, Nina?" When she didn't answer right away, he said, "You don't have to tell me if it's too painful to talk about."

She shrugged, turning her gaze back to the window. "There's nothing much to tell. When I was fifteen, a wealthy older couple decided to adopt me. They took me into their home, decorated a beautiful room for me, bought me expensive clothes, gave me everything I could possibly want. For a while, they treated me like a princess. I thought it was too good to be true, and it was. A few months before the adoption became final, they decided they didn't want me after all." There was a little more to the story than that, but Nina didn't particularly want to go into the details. Instead she glanced at Grant. "They took me back to the orphanage and left me."

Something flickered in his eyes. Sympathy? Pity? Suspicion? "Why?"

Nina shrugged again. "They had their reasons."

"It must have been hard for you."

"Not really. The nuns were very good to me. I was glad to go back."

"You don't know anything about your real mother and father?" Grant never took his eyes off her. Nina couldn't imagine what he was thinking. Was he wondering why no one had ever wanted her—not her real parents, not the older couple who had almost adopted her and certainly not the Fairchilds?

Nina had wondered the same thing herself until Dustin had come along, and then, as she'd stared down into his precious little face, the realization had come to her that the question no longer mattered. As Dustin's mother, she was complete and whole and very much wanted, and she had thought no one could ever take that feeling away from her. But someone had.

"I don't know anything about my real parents," she said at last. "The nuns found me outside the convent gates one morning. I was only a few weeks old. There wasn't a clue to my real identity. One of the sisters named me Nina after her mother, and Sparrow because she said sparrows carry the souls of unborn children to earth and I had been given a very special soul. One that was capable of great...love.''

Without warning, Grant reached across the table and took her hand. Nina wanted to pull away from him, but something kept her still. That same something made her fingers tremble beneath his, made her long to have his arms close around her, to draw strength from his nearness.

He stroked her knuckles with his thumb. ''You've had a hard time of it,'' he said softly.

''Others have had a lot worse.''

He smiled, but his eyes remained dark. ''You make me want to take care of you.''

Nina glanced at him in surprise, shivering at his words. ''I don't need taking care of. I can take care of myself.''

His grip on her fingers tightened ever so slightly. ''I know. And that makes you even more desirable. Your independence and fierce determination mixed with an incredible softness and vulnerability. It's a lethal combination, Nina.''

''But I'm not vulnerable.'' She did withdraw her hand then and laced her fingers together in her lap. But her skin still tingled from where he had held her. Nina wanted to deny the sensation, but couldn't. She closed her eyes briefly. ''I'm not vulnerable,'' she repeated, almost to herself.

''We're all vulnerable. We all have weaknesses. Each and every one of us.''

Not you, she thought. She'd never met anyone with such strength. Such presence. How could someone like Grant Chambers be vulnerable?

The waitress brought the check then, and without

a word, Grant withdrew a credit card from his wallet and tossed it on the table. They didn't speak again until after he'd signed the receipt. "Let's get out of here," he said.

He took her elbow as they left the restaurant, and once again Nina knew she should pull away from his closeness. At some point, they were going to have to address what was happening between them, and once that discussion took place, everything would change. Nina would no longer be able to pretend that Grant's relationship to her son was their only connection.

Outside, sunset had faded to dusk. A glimmer of starlight shone through patches of clouds over the water. The evening was warm and still, and the sound of the surf filled Nina with a melancholy she wasn't sure she understood.

Grant glanced at his watch. "It's still too early to meet Ruthanne. How about a walk on the beach? It's been a long time since I've done that."

In her present mood, Nina wasn't sure more time alone with Grant was such a good idea, but she shrugged and nodded.

"I need to call the office first," he said.

"This late? It's nearly six. Will someone still be in?"

"Six o'clock is early around there," he said dryly. "I don't usually get out of the office before seven or eight." At the bottom of the wooden steps that led from the restaurant's outdoor deck to the beach, Grant took out his cellular phone. "I'll just be a minute."

Nina took that as her cue to walk away. She headed for the surf, removing her shoes and socks and rolling up her jeans so she could sample the water. The night was mild, but the gulf waters were frigid. Shivering, she quickly retreated to dry sand and sat down, watching the rhythmic rise and fall of the swells. By the time she'd put back on her shoes and socks, Grant had joined her.

"Water cold?" He sat down beside her, their shoulders almost brushing.

Nina's heart raced in spite of her efforts to calm it. "Too cold for me."

Moonbeams played across the water, silvering the waves with a beautiful, incandescent glow. Nina slanted a glance at Grant, studying his profile in the pale light, thinking that of all the men she might have fallen in love with, the one who threatened to steal her heart was the one who had the power to keep her from her son.

I'm not in love with you, she silently vowed. *I can't be.*

As if she'd spoken the words aloud, Grant turned to her suddenly. His expression was enigmatic in the moonlight, his gaze so deep, butterflies trembled in Nina's stomach. The attraction between them was suddenly electric, and Nina knew that in another moment, he would kiss her and she would let him. And then she would be lost, because she would no longer be able to think with her head instead of her heart.

She couldn't let that happen. No matter what it cost her, she could not let down her defenses.

She turned back to the ocean, trying to break the almost unbearable tension between them. "Why did you go to Venezuela?" she asked, searching for a harmless topic of conversation.

Beside her, Grant stirred impatiently. "I was sent to Venezuela. Exiled, you might say."

Nina turned back to him in surprise. "Why?"

He shrugged. "I was involved in a scandal. Nothing earth-shattering, but the oil industry is like a small town in many respects. Rumors and innuendos can take on monumental proportions, and a person's reputation can affect a business deal in ways you can't even begin to imagine." His tone grew bitter, and it occurred to Nina that maybe she'd been wrong about him earlier. Maybe he *was* vulnerable.

"What happened?"

"There was a woman, of course." The bitterness in his voice turned to irony. He glanced at her in the moonlight.

"Of course," Nina murmured, but she felt a tiny stab of jealousy at the thought of Grant being involved with another woman. Which was foolish because there had undoubtedly been dozens of other women. Nina wasn't yet one of them, and if she was smart, she never would be.

"We had a brief fling in college," he explained. "Nothing serious. A few dates, then we went our separate ways. Four years ago, she turned up in Houston with a ten-year-old son she said was mine. She wanted money. A one-time payoff and I'd never hear from her again. Otherwise, she would tell anyone who would listen to her that I had known about the pregnancy and had refused to support my child."

Nina wondered if that was why he was having such a hard time accepting what she'd told him about John David. Because of his past experience, was he automatically distrustful of women making claims about children?

"What did you do?" she asked.

"The company was in the middle of a merger with

a very old and very conservative company. Their board had made it clear that family values were just as important to them as business ethics, and they were, frankly, a little worried about both in regards to Chambers Petroleum. Somehow my father managed to convince them we were the very epitome of respectability, and the negotiations proceeded. When he found out about the woman, he nearly hit the roof. He insisted that I pay her off before Trident's board found out about her.''

"And?"

Grant shrugged. "And I refused. I told him that if the child was mine, he deserved more than a payoff. I'd want to pay child support, set up a trust fund for his education, that sort of thing. And I'd want to get to know him, be a part of his life, maybe even try to be a father to him.''

Nina sat watching Grant and thinking that in so many ways, he was still a stranger to her. Yet the way he talked about the child and the way he opened up to Nina drew her into his orbit, made her powerless to resist the pull he exerted on her. He was no longer the enemy, no longer a man to be feared, but a man she could admire. A man she understood. A man she wanted to know better.

"You wanted him to be your son, didn't you?" she asked quietly.

It was his turn to be surprised. "Funny you should say that. It never even occurred to my father that I might actually want the kid to be mine." He paused. "It's hard to explain, but the moment I looked into that boy's eyes, I saw a part of me staring back. A part of me that had never connected with my father the way I'd want my son to connect with me. And I didn't want that for him. Does that make sense?''

"Yes." Nina drew her legs up and hugged her knees. "I know exactly what you mean. You always want for your children the thing you wanted most for yourself and didn't have. I wanted so badly for my baby to grow up knowing he was loved, knowing he had a mother who would always be there for him.'' Tears stung Nina's eyes, and she turned away, resting her chin on her knees as she watched the ebb and flow of the tide. She could feel Grant's gaze on her, but she didn't turn back. She couldn't.

"You'll be a wonderful mother," he said softly. "You *are* a wonderful mother."

His words touched Nina in a way she couldn't explain. She wiped the moisture from her face with the back of her hand. "Thank you for saying that."

She felt Grant's hand in her hair, and she did turn to him then. Their gazes met in the moonlight, and a wave of emotion swept over her. He cupped the back of her neck with his hand, and in another moment, Nina knew he would pull her to him. She closed her eyes, letting the sensation of his touch fill her with anticipation. With a desire she would never have thought possible.

"What happened with the little boy?" she asked, knowing she was merely prolonging the moment.

Grant's hand slipped from her hair, and his voice hardened. "The lawyers got involved. Tests were performed."

Nina glanced at him. "DNA tests?"

"It didn't come to that. A blood test proved I couldn't be the father." He watched her in the moonlight, and Nina wondered if he was comparing his situation to hers. Then he shrugged. "The woman made up the story in order to extort money from me. I've always suspected someone who wanted to undermine my position in the company found her and helped her concoct the whole thing. The boy was just an innocent victim in all of it." Grant paused. "Trident got wind of the story and pulled out of the merger. Because I didn't handle the situation the way my father wanted me to, he decided to send me to Venezuela."

"I'm sorry," Nina said, not knowing what else to say.

"The little boy was the one I felt sorry for," Grant said. "I couldn't help thinking that if he had been my son, we would have lost out on all those years together. That would have been very sad."

"It's more than sad to lose time with your child," Nina said. "It's devastating." Before he could answer her, she rose, brushing the sand off the seat of her jeans. "It's nearly seven. We should probably get going."

Grant stood, too, but when Nina turned to head back to the car, he put his hands on her shoulders and turned her to face him. "I'm sorry about your baby. I'm sorry for everything that's happened to you. But I swear, I'll do everything in my power to help you find him."

"I want to believe that," she whispered, "but how can I?"

His gaze deepened on her. "Because I care about you."

"Why?"

He brushed a knuckle down the side of her face. "Because you're you. Because you're Nina." When she said nothing to that—when she *couldn't* say anything—his grasp tightened almost imperceptibly on her shoulders. "I think I'm falling in love with you."

He couldn't have shocked her more. Nina's breath caught in her throat as her heart pounded in long, painful strokes against her chest. "I don't know what to say to that."

He smiled, but his eyes remained dark, his expression serious. "You don't have to say anything. I just thought you should know how I feel."

Nina's whole being churned with confusion. She was experienced enough to know that Grant was attracted to her, that he wanted her. But love? Could he really fall in love with her, knowing what he knew about her? *Not* knowing what would happen in the future? Could love be that powerful? Could it really conquer all?

As much as Nina wanted to believe it was so, she didn't dare.

She shook her head sadly. "Nothing has changed for us. I still believe your sister stole my baby, and I'm still going to do everything in my power to get him back."

"I know that. And I'll still do whatever I can to protect Vanessa, but that doesn't change the way I feel about you." A brief smile touched his lips. "But I can't deny I wish we'd met under different circumstances."

"If it weren't for the circumstances, we wouldn't have met at all," Nina said.

His hands were still on her shoulders, and he pulled her to him ever so slightly. "I don't believe that. Some things are meant to be."

"And some things aren't." But her words weren't very convincing.

They were standing very close now, and Nina wondered if he could hear the pounding of her heart, if he could sense the turmoil of her emotions, the weaknesses in her defense.

Very gently, he took her chin in his hand, lifting her face to stare deeply into her eyes. For the longest moment, neither of them said anything; neither of them moved. They stood locked in a timeless moment of expectation. Of longing. And then, not so gently, Grant lowered his head and kissed her.

Nina closed her eyes as his lips touched hers and his arms came around her to pull her close. She put her hands on his chest, to push him away at first, and then, as the kiss deepened, to steady herself against him.

A thrill of excitement raced through her. She had never felt this way before, never experienced this exquisite sense of inevitability.

Behind them, the surf pounded against the beach. Above them, the moon cast a pale, intimate glow upon the water. And beneath Nina's hand, Grant's heart beat a rhythm as wild and frenzied as her own.

You've never thrown caution to the wind? he'd once asked her. *Never been swept away by passion?*

Was this what he'd meant, then? This longing, this hunger, this desperation to have him kiss her and keep on kissing her, to have his hands all over her, to have him pull her body closer and closer until...

He feathered kisses over her face, weaving his hands through her hair, whispering to her until nothing else seemed to matter. Until Nina couldn't quite remember why she shouldn't fall in love with this man.

"I would do anything for you," he murmured against her ear, and Nina felt a thrill of power race through her.

"Anything?" she breathed.

"You know I would."

His tongue caressed the shell of her ear, and Nina shivered.

"Would you...?" She felt the slightest hesitation on his part before she could finish what she'd been about to say. His hands slipped from her hair to her shoulders, holding her close but with a subtle distance that filled Nina with regret.

Desire glinted in his eyes, but now another emotion darkened his gaze, as well. Almost in challenge, he said, "Would I what, Nina?"

She closed her eyes, wanting to draw him back to her, wanting to recapture the moment when the pain and grief of the past six months had faded. When everything in the world had disappeared but the two of them. But Nina couldn't bring that moment back, and she knew it. There would never be just the two of them.

It was almost a relief to feel the pain of her loss return. To realize that nothing, not even a man like Grant Chambers, could make her forget what she had to do.

She met his gaze and said, "Would you let me see my son?"

His hands dropped from her shoulders as he continued to stare down at her. He suddenly looked dark and remote, much as he'd looked in the park the day he'd taken her baby from her arms. Nina shivered, thinking that no matter what he said to the contrary, he was her enemy.

"I'll see what I can do," he said unexpectedly. His voice, so cold and distant, made chill bumps rise on Nina's skin.

She wrapped her arms around her middle. "You'd...do that for me?"

"Why do you look so surprised? I said I'd do anything for you, and you called me on it."

He turned to go, but Nina caught his arm. He glanced down at her hand, then back up into her face. One dark brow rose in question.

"You don't know how much it would mean to me to see Dustin again."

"The baby's name is John David. And like I said, I'll see what I can do. I always try to keep my word, whether you believe it or not."

And with that, he turned and headed back to the car.

WHEN THEY ARRIVED at Smith Street, where the café Ruthanne Keller had told them about was located, the first thing Nina saw were the flashing lights on three police cars and an EMT vehicle parked midway down the street. Grant located a parking spot and pulled to the curb.

"I wonder what's going on?" she asked as he straightened the car in the space.

"I don't know." He killed the engine and turned to her. A look of awareness passed between them, one Nina tried to ignore. Her senses were still filled with the scene on the beach, but it had been painfully obvious to her from the beginning that there could never be a relationship between her and Grant. Now he knew it, too. He knew where her priorities lay, and Nina was glad. It was better to have everything out in the open.

Still, as they got out of the car and headed down the street toward the café, she couldn't help being conscious of the way her pulse pounded at Grant's nearness, or of the shiver that prickled through her when he brushed against her arm.

She wondered if he was still upset with her for using his feelings for her—his *professed* feelings—to get what she wanted. Nina wasn't particularly proud of what she'd done, but if she could see her son again, hold him in her arms again, she knew she would have no regrets.

Well, maybe one or two, she acknowledged, slanting a glance up at Grant. His expression gave away nothing of what he was feeling. The past few minutes might never have happened. His eyes were glued to the street and to the flashing lights ahead of them.

A crowd had formed on the street in front of Antoinette's. The police cars and ambulance were directly in front of the café, and a semicircle of pedestrians blocked Nina's view. Grant walked up to the nearest bystander and asked him what had happened.

"Hit-and-run," the man said grimly. "I saw the whole thing. Damn car came out of nowhere. Mowed her down and just kept going. She never even knew what hit her."

A sick feeling curled in Nina's stomach. She heard Grant ask, "Did you know her?"

The man shrugged. "I saw her around. She was a regular at the café." He angled a nod toward Antoinette's. The sick feeling in Nina's stomach turned to one of dread. She and Grant exchanged a glance before he turned back to the man at his side.

"Did you know her name?"

"Ruth, Ruthie, something like that. She was a nurse, I think."

Nina put a hand to her mouth, not wanting to believe what she'd just heard, or the implications of what had just happened. As the EMTs picked up the stretcher from the street, the crowd moved back, parting for a split second so that Nina caught a glimpse of the blood-soaked sheet completely covering the victim's body.

Ruthanne Keller, the only person other than Nina who could identify Karen Smith, was dead.

Chapter Eleven

The house was dark when Grant pulled into Nina's driveway. She'd forgotten to leave a light on when they'd left, and now the place seemed cold and forbidding to her, almost frightening.

Grant turned off the engine and shut off the headlights. Darkness fell around them, and Nina shivered, remembering Ruthanne Keller's cold, lifeless body being lifted into the ambulance.

A hit-and-run, the man at the scene had told them. A car had come out of nowhere, struck her down, then zoomed away. Was it merely a coincidence that Ruthanne had been killed minutes before she would have met with Nina and Grant? A coincidence that she had seen something in Vanessa Baldwin's picture that had disturbed her?

Another thought occurred to Nina. Grant had made a phone call before they'd walked on the beach. She didn't know whom he'd talked to, but what if he'd made arrangements to have Ruthanne taken care of?

Nina darted a glance at Grant. He was watching her quietly in the shadowed light from the street, and she shuddered, wondering what he was thinking. What he was planning.

Don't be ridiculous, she scolded herself. *He's not that kind of man.*

He wouldn't do anything so cold-blooded as to order someone's death…but how could she really be sure of that? Nina knew very little about Grant, only that he was very protective of his sister, and he would do anything to keep her from getting hurt.

Did that mean pretending to fall in love with Nina? Could she really trust his earlier declaration of love?

"What's wrong?"

The sound of his voice caused Nina to start. Chill bumps rose on her arms. "I was just thinking about poor Ruthanne. If we hadn't asked her to meet us tonight, she might still be alive."

"You don't know that. She said she went to the café often for dinner before going home. Chances are she would have gone there anyway, even if she hadn't been meeting with us."

"I suppose so," Nina murmured, but she still wasn't convinced. "You have to admit, it's a very strange coincidence. She was on duty the night I gave birth. She saw the woman I knew as Karen Smith at the hospital. I keep asking myself, who would want Ruthanne dead? And the answer I keep coming up with is someone who was afraid of being identified by her."

"I'm not sure I like what you're getting at here," Grant said slowly. "You're surely not suggesting Vanessa had anything to do with Ruthanne's death."

"I don't know," Nina said. "You saw her reaction to the picture we showed her."

"That picture was no proof, and you know it." Grant ran a hand through his hair in frustration. "You're making too much of this. Ruthanne's death was just a tragic accident. They happen all the time. Can't you accept that?''

''No, I can't. And deep down, I don't think you can, either.'' When he said nothing, Nina drew a long breath and released it. ''It's been a long day. I should go in.''

''I'll walk you to the door.''

''That's not necessary—'' But he was already getting out of the car, and Nina wasn't sure whether to feel frightened or grateful. The thought of going into her cold, dark house alone was not exactly comforting, but neither were her thoughts about Grant.

He couldn't have had anything to do with the accident, she thought as they climbed her porch steps and she unlocked her front door. She couldn't believe a man who had been so passionate and tender earlier could deliberately have set such a tragedy in motion. Grant was innocent in all this. Nina wanted to believe that more than anything.

He waited until she'd stepped inside the door and turned on the light, then he leaned against the door frame, staring down at her. He looked as if he wanted to take her in his arms again and kiss her until all the darkness faded. Until all her doubts about him vanished. In spite of her chaotic thoughts, excitement shot through her.

Inadvertently she took a step back from him, and something flashed in his eyes.

''About tonight,'' he said. ''Earlier on the beach—''

Nina made a dismissive gesture with her hand. ''You don't have to explain. I know it was a mistake.''

''Was it?'' He stared down at her. ''I meant what

I said, Nina. I care about you. Probably more than I should under the circumstances. I would never intentionally hurt you.''

''But you have to protect your sister. I do understand, Grant.''

''I wonder if you do.'' He hesitated, his expression grim. ''I have to do what's right, no matter how I feel about you. A lot of lives are at stake here.''

''We both know what's right,'' Nina said with an edge of bitterness. ''It's right for me to have my son back.''

''I'm not arguing with that.''

''Even if John David turns out to be my son?''

He stared at her for a long moment without answering. Then he nodded. ''Even if John David turns out to be your son.''

Nina was speechless. His words blew her away. Was he serious? Did he really mean it?

''I would never keep you from your baby, Nina. You have to believe that.''

''I…want to,'' she whispered. ''You don't know how badly.'' When she looked up at him, she could almost believe everything would be all right. That she would get her son back, and Grant would help her. She wanted to tell him how much his words meant to her, and of the hope surging through her at that moment.

She reached out to touch his arm, but before she made contact, his cellular phone rang, and Nina let her hand drop to her side, the moment lost.

Regret settled over her as she watched him remove the tiny phone from his jacket pocket and put it to his ear. His expression grew even more grim as he listened for a moment, then said, "I'll be right there."

Nina knew immediately something was wrong. Her heart plunged as Grant put away the phone. "What's wrong?" she asked in dread. "Is it the baby?"

"John David's fine. That was my sister's housekeeper. Vanessa's in the hospital. She collapsed at home earlier this evening."

Nina gasped. "Oh, my God. I'm so sorry. I-is she going to be all right?"

Grant shrugged, his expression closed. "I don't know. I have to get to the hospital."

"Yes, of course." Nina put trembling fingers to her lips, trying not to think beyond the moment, but she couldn't help it. Questions welled inside her. Did this clear Vanessa, then? Did this mean she had nothing to do with Ruthanne Keller's death?

No matter what the answers to those questions were, Nina would not have wished this on Vanessa. And especially not on Grant. She knew how close he and his sister were and what this must be doing to him.

"Grant, I am sorry," she said. "I truly hope your sister will be all right."

His gaze was uncertain, as if he didn't know whether or not to believe her. Then he said, "I'll be in touch," and strode down the porch steps to disappear into the darkness of the front yard.

WHEN GRANT GOT to the hospital, his father had just arrived as well. They stood in the corridor outside Vanessa's room in the cardiac-care unit, gazing at her through the glass partition.

She looked pale and very fragile lying against the white sheets. An IV needle dripped medication into her veins while tubes inserted into her nostrils helped her breathe. A monitor near her bed showed the weak, irregular pattern of her heartbeat.

"Dear God," J.D. whispered. He pressed the glass with his fingertips, as if he could somehow reach through and make contact with Vanessa. As if he could somehow will his strength into her.

Grant and his father had never had an easy relationship, but Grant tried to put all that behind him now, just as he always had in times of crisis. He gripped his father's shoulder. "She'll be all right. She's come through this before. Vanessa has always been a fighter."

J.D. nodded, but worry had etched deep lines in his face. Grant had never thought of his father as old, but he seemed that way now. Old and frail and defeated.

His father drew a long, shaky breath. "She looks like her mother lying there."

Grant had very few memories of his mother. She'd died of cancer when he was five and Vanessa was barely one. As the years went by, he could hardly even remember what she'd looked like, but an image came to him now of a woman dressed all in white, a woman with the sweetest smile he'd ever seen and the softest voice he'd ever heard. He could almost feel her comforting hand upon his brow.

For some reason, the memory made him think of Nina. Of the love she had for her own son.

"What happened?" he asked his father.

"I was out all evening. I had a meeting that ran late, and when I got home a little while ago, there was a message on my machine from Vanessa's housekeeper. Apparently Vanessa collapsed at home earlier. Alice Becker found her unconscious in the nursery. Alice called the paramedics, then began CPR...." He trailed off, shaking his head. "That woman has always irritated the hell out of me, but she did something right tonight. She saved Vanessa's life. When I think how close we came to dismissing her..."

And Grant had been the main one who had wanted Alice Becker fired. If he'd had his way, she would have been canned the night he'd found out about her drinking, but Vanessa had kept the woman on, and now she'd saved his sister's life. Grant wondered what message, if any, he should derive from that irony. In any case, he was grateful to the woman.

"Do you have any idea what brought on the attack?" he asked.

But before his father could answer, someone called J.D.'s name, and they both turned to see Clayton rushing down the corridor toward them. He looked uncharacteristically disheveled. His tie was loosened and his blond hair, usually so carefully styled, looked as if he'd been running his fingers through it. Or someone had, Grant thought dryly.

"I got here as soon as I heard," he told J.D., self-consciously adjusting his tie.

He had yet to glance through the window at Vanessa. So much for husbandly devotion, Grant thought. He couldn't help wondering where Clayton had been all evening, or what he'd been up to. He had the look of a man with a guilty conscience, and was trying like hell to hide it.

As if reading Grant's thoughts, Clayton whirled to

stare at Vanessa through the window. "Oh, dear God," he said in a ragged voice. "My poor Van."

It was enough to turn Grant's stomach. He glanced away, not able to make eye contact with his brother-in-law.

"What happened?" Clayton asked in anguish.

J.D. went through the scenario again, and when he finished, he said impatiently, "I'm going to find the doctor. I can't stand this damn waiting. They've got to tell us something."

After he'd disappeared down the corridor, Clayton stood staring through the window at Vanessa. "She has to be all right," he muttered. "She *has* to be."

Unable to resist, Grant said, "You can save the act. My father isn't around to hear you."

Clayton turned on him, his eyes icy with contempt. "Damn you. How dare you question my devotion to Vanessa when this is all your fault. I'm sure your father realizes that, too."

Grant lifted a brow. "*My* fault? How do you figure that?"

Clayton shrugged. "Vanessa's been under a terrible strain since that woman showed up at our house, making all those crazy claims. It was your responsibility to take care of her, but of course you didn't, or couldn't, and now look what's happened. Maybe you should start cleaning out your office and packing your bags, Grant. I think you've proved yourself to your father yet again. Proved what a failure you are, that is."

Grant shook his head in disgust. "I can't believe you. Your wife may be dying, and all you can think about is how to get rid of me? What the hell is the matter with you?"

Anger twisted Clayton's mouth. "We were crazy to ever listen to you. I should have taken care of that woman myself. I should have paid her off right from the start, and none of this ever would have happened."

"I told you before, Nina doesn't want money. She's convinced John David is her son, and nothing you could have offered her would have made her go away."

"And nothing you've done has cleared this mess up, either, now has it?" Clayton demanded. "Let me tell you something, Grant. If anything happens to Vanessa...if she doesn't pull through this, I'm holding you personally responsible."

Grant felt the heat of his anger crawl through him. His fists balled at his sides, but his voice remained deadly calm. "If you're so concerned about my sister, why weren't you home with her tonight? Why was Alice Becker the one to find her and not you?"

Something flashed across Clayton's face. A look of guilt? Grant was more convinced than ever that his brother-in-law was hiding something.

But Clayton was a master at turning the tables. He smiled coldly. "As long as we're conducting an inquisition here, why don't you tell me how you spent your day? Lori said you left the office just after lunch and didn't tell her where you were going. I think your father would probably like to hear this, too."

Contemptuous satisfaction glittered in Clayton's eyes when Grant hesitated. *He knows,* Grant thought. *The bastard already knows where I was.*

"I was with Nina all afternoon. We drove down to Galveston to talk to the detective who's investigating her son's disappearance. But then, of course, you already knew that, didn't you, Clayton? What did you do, follow us down there?''

Clayton smirked. ''I have better things to do with my time—like work, for instance. It may interest you to know that I spent a good deal of my day with the Ventura people. I've always had the best interests of the company at heart, as your father well knows. I'm willing to do whatever it takes to see this merger go through whether you are or not.''

As usual, Clayton's timing was impeccable. J.D. walked up beside him and put a comforting hand on his shoulder.

Clayton turned back to the window to stare sadly at Vanessa. ''But I can't think about business now. I can't think about anything but Vanessa. She and John David are my life. If I were ever to lose either of them…'' He trailed off, closing his eyes as if overcome with emotion.

J.D. patted Clayton's shoulder. ''She'll be all right, son, don't worry. You're not going to lose Vanessa or John David. I'll see to that.''

Grant might have been relieved to see the return of his father's arrogance if not for the fact that he was so obviously being taken in by Clayton. But what could Grant say? Clayton was J.D.'s fair-haired boy, and he wouldn't expect or want criticism from Grant. And he certainly would not want Clayton's true nature exposed because that would reflect badly upon himself. Grant knew his father all too well, so he said nothing.

But it's not over, he thought. *Not by a long shot.* This time he wouldn't go quietly off to the ends of the earth. This time he would damn well stay and fight.

"Come on, let's take a walk," J.D. said to Clayton. "It'll do you good."

Clayton nodded. But he couldn't resist flashing Grant a look of triumph before turning and following his father-in-law down the corridor.

Alone at the window, Grant stood staring at his sister, but his thoughts were still on Clayton. His brother-in-law's last words disturbed him in a way he didn't understand. *I can't think of anything but Vanessa. She and John David are my life. If I were to lose either of them…*

Grant knew Clayton's distress had been an act for J.D.'s benefit, but there was something about his choice of words that was worrisome. What *would* happen if Clayton did lose Vanessa and John David? Clayton's meteoric rise at Chambers Petroleum could be directly linked to his marriage to Vanessa, and even more so to the birth of J.D.'s only grandson.

But if Vanessa and John David were out of the picture, what would happen then? Clayton's position in the company would be severely weakened. Without the familial connection, he would have very little chance of being named CEO, and Grant had no doubt the thought had occurred to Clayton, as well.

Was that the reason he felt so threatened by Nina? Was he worried she might somehow manage to prove the baby was hers?

Now you're thinking crazy, Grant told himself.

There was no way his sister's child could be Nina's. He'd seen a picture of Vanessa while she'd been pregnant. He'd spoken with her doctor.

That man was lying, Nina had told him after they'd left Dr. Mapleton's office. *Couldn't you tell?*

Was it possible?

Grant shook his head, trying to clear his thoughts. Of course it wasn't possible, and yet he knew Nina wasn't crazy. He'd never met a saner person in his life.

And there was another thing Grant knew without a doubt. No matter what Sergeant Farrell had inferred earlier, Nina would never, ever hurt her own child. Neither would she have willingly given him up. She loved him more than anything in the world and was desperate to get him back.

So where did that leave Grant? Did he trust in Nina, a woman who appealed to him in ways he couldn't begin to explain, or did he trust in his sister, a woman who was fighting for her life? A woman he thought he knew as well as he knew himself.

His sister wasn't perfect. Grant had never deluded himself in that regard. She was spoiled and moody and when pressed, could be extremely manipulative. But to steal another woman's child…

A DNA test would clear everything up, a voice whispered inside him.

Guilt stabbed through Grant as he stood staring at his sister through the window. He remembered the fun they'd had as children, the closeness they'd shared as teenagers. Theirs had been a very special bond—Vanessa, the beautiful, frail sister who, if truth be told, had made Grant feel strong and important in his protectiveness of her.

He felt that same protectiveness now as he stood watching her fight for her life, and an overwhelming sadness came over him. Vanessa or Nina. How could he choose without losing something precious? Without betraying someone very special to him?

No matter how Grant looked at the situation, he

could find no happy ending to this story. And as much as he didn't want to think about it, he couldn't deny the fact that a woman connected to Nina and her baby's disappearance had been killed tonight. He wanted more than anything to believe it was a tragic coincidence, but Grant wasn't stupid. The possibility, no matter how remote, existed that Ruthanne Keller's death had not been an accident.

SOMETIME AFTER MIDNIGHT, Nina awakened with a terrifying sense of déjà vu. Had she been having a nightmare? Was that why a faint scent of smoke seemed to linger on the air?

She sprang up in bed. *My God,* she thought. The smell was real!

Jumping to her feet, she rushed across the room to the bedroom door, cautiously testing the knob to make sure it wasn't hot. She opened the door slowly, stepping into the hallway. The scent seemed to have disappeared out here, and Nina thought for a moment she had imagined it. But then the smoke alarm at the back of the house began to blare, and her heart leaped to her throat. Her house was on fire!

Images of another fire shot through her, and Nina fled down the hallway. In her blind panic, she tripped over the hem of her nightgown and went sprawling to the floor. Heart pounding, she struggled to her feet only to realize that the smoke alarm near her bedroom was still silent, which meant the fire had to be at the back of the house. That was why there wasn't much smoke in the hallway. Nina had plenty of time to get out of the house. There was no need to panic.

She drew a long breath, willing herself to calm

down. If the fire was in the back, she would need to go out the front door. It was as simple as that.

Pausing in the living room only long enough to grab her cordless phone, Nina hurried outside. She dialed 911, reporting the fire and her address to the dispatcher, then rushed around to the back of the house, careful to keep a safe distance.

She could hear the alarm blasting inside, but there still wasn't much smoke, even back here. Nina wondered if she might have overreacted, if she should have checked the house herself before calling the fire department.

Her office was located at the very back of the house, in what had once been a sun porch. Tentatively Nina approached the back door. There didn't seem to be much danger. She could see into her office through the glass panel. The smoke was minimal, and she could see no flames. Perhaps one of the electrical cords to her computer equipment had shorted out. Maybe she should go back inside and—

Suddenly with a whooshing sound that stole Nina's breath, the whole room erupted into flames. The intense heat rocked her backward. She stumbled away from the fire, coughing and sputtering as her heart pounded in terror.

Within seconds her office was completely ablaze. Her computer, her files and all her work were being destroyed, and she could do nothing but stand by and watch.

Motivated by desperation, she glanced around, searching for and finding the water hose connected to the faucet beside her garage.

Rushing over, she turned on the water and dragged the hose toward the house, aiming the nozzle at the fire. Black smoke billowed into the air where water met flame, and the windows in her office began to shatter. The battle seemed hopeless, but she wasn't about to give up without a fight.

In no more than five minutes from when she'd called, she heard the sound of a siren as a fire engine entered her neighborhood. Moments later the truck pulled up outside her house, and the firemen took over. Nina relinquished the hose and retreated to the garage, watching the tableau with a numbness she knew wouldn't last.

In an amazingly short period of time, the blaze was subdued, but her office was little more than a smoldering mass of rubble. One of the firemen came over and spoke with her. "You're lucky. The fire was contained to just that one room. You'll have some smoke and water damage to contend with, but it could have been a lot worse."

Nina nodded, not feeling very lucky at the moment. She stared at her office, thinking of everything that had been lost.

"Ma'am, do you have any idea how the fire started?"

Nina shook her head. "Not really. But it's an old house. The wiring could be faulty."

"You didn't leave a cigarette or candle burning, a space heater going, anything like that?"

Again Nina shook her head. She wrapped her arms around her middle as the numbness began to wear off. "No, it couldn't have been anything like that. I don't smoke, and I'm a very careful person."

He nodded. "Well, we'll know more when the arson investigators are finished."

Nina looked at him in shock. "Arson investigators? You think someone deliberately set my house on fire?''

''Probably not. Most home fires are accidental, but an investigation is routine.'' He started to walk away, then came back over. ''By the way, do you usually keep the back door locked?''

''Of course I do. That room is my office. I have...*had* a lot of expensive equipment in there. Why?''

He hesitated. ''It wasn't locked when we entered.''

Nina's heart thudded against her chest. ''Then you *don't* think the fire was an accident, do you?''

Again he hesitated. ''Let's wait and see what the investigators have to say.''

Nina followed him back to the house, but when she would have entered the rubble-filled room, he said, ''Ma'am, you're not wearing shoes. There's glass everywhere, not to mention a lot of other debris. You could get hurt in there.''

For the first time, Nina realized she was still in her nightgown. The night chill seeped through her. ''I know, but I just wanted to see—''

She caught a glimpse of her office and gasped in dismay. What the fire hadn't got, the water had. Everything was completely destroyed. Her computer, her files, everything. Luckily she'd recently bought another computer and installed it in her bedroom, so that she could work in the middle of the night when she couldn't sleep. Most of her current projects were also stored on that machine, but all her files and records—so much time and energy—were gone.

Tears stung behind her lids. Nina supposed she should be grateful that she, unlike most people, possessed hardly any irreplaceable photographs or me-

mentos. As it was, her greatest personal loss was all the records and files she'd accumulated concerning Dustin's disappearance—the private investigator's reports, copies of the letters she'd written, virtually everything concerning her son.

Everything.

The revelation hit her so suddenly, Nina actually swayed. The fireman caught her elbow, steadying her. "Easy now. It's always a blow."

For a moment, Nina couldn't catch her breath. Waves of shock washed over her. Someone had done this to her. Someone had deliberately destroyed everything she had connected with her baby.

Dear God.

Lies were being told about her. Records and files had been destroyed. And Ruthanne Keller was dead.

What would be next? Nina thought. *Who* would be next? How far was someone willing to go to keep her from her son?

Chapter Twelve

Grant spent most of the night at the hospital and only went home the next morning long enough to shower and change clothes before going into the office. Vanessa had taken a dramatic turn for the better just before midnight, and Grant persuaded his father to go home and get some rest. Clayton left, too, and Grant was allowed inside Vanessa's room to sit by her bed for the remainder of the night.

She awakened in the morning and smiled at him before drifting back to sleep. Grant took that as a good sign, and decided to go into work after all. He knew both his father and Clayton were planning to spend the morning at the hospital, so someone needed to hold down the fort.

He was hoping to knock out the mountain of paperwork that had accumulated on his desk the past few days, but when he opened the door to his secretary's office, Trent Fairchild was waiting for him. He reclined in Lori's chair, his feet propped on her desk as he read the paper. When he heard Grant open the door, he put aside the paper and rose.

"Hell, it's about time you dragged yourself in here," he grumbled. "Same old Grant, I see. Keeping banker's hours while the rest of us work our butts off.''

''As if you've ever broken a sweat in your life,'' Grant said. The two men shook hands.

''Good to see you, buddy,'' Trent said, clasping Grant's shoulder.

''You, too.'' Grant unlocked the door to his office, and Trent followed him in.

''Venezuela seems to have agreed with you.'' Trent sprawled in a chair opposite Grant's desk. ''You don't look any worse for the wear.''

Grant wished he could say the same thing about Trent. Grant hadn't seen his friend in over four years, but the outward changes were quite dramatic. Trent's dark hair was peppered with gray, and the lines around his mouth and eyes were deeper than they should have been for his thirty-two years. Trent had always loved to party, and it seemed to Grant that all those late nights were catching up with a vengeance.

''So.'' He sat down behind his desk. ''What brings you to Houston this early in the morning? You must have left San Antonio before dawn.''

''Nope.'' Trent folded his arms across his chest. ''I spent the night here in town with a friend. I tried to call you last night, but you weren't home. Or at least you weren't answering your phone. Figured you were probably entertaining,'' he said with a sly grin.

Grant frowned. ''You don't know about Vanessa, then. She was taken to the hospital last night.''

Trent immediately sobered. ''Is it her heart? Is she going to be all right?''

''She's doing much better this morning, thank God. Her doctors are cautiously optimistic.''

"Well, that's good." Trent shook his head. "It's a damn shame, all that poor girl's been through. And now this thing with Nina."

Grant glanced at him warily. "I take it that's why you're here."

Trent shifted in his chair. Some indefinable emotion flashed in his eyes. "Mother told me she'd talked to you the other night. I expected you to call me back, but when I didn't hear from you, I thought I'd better hightail it over here and give you the lowdown."

"Your mother told me you had Nina investigated before she and Garrett were married," Grant said. "Edwina said you'd found out something disturbing about an adoption that didn't go through."

"You bet I did." Trent crossed an ankle over his knee, displaying a gray ostrich-skin cowboy boot. "When Nina was fifteen, some rich old couple decided to adopt her. They'd never been able to have kids of their own. Because of their age, they didn't want a baby or a young child, but they convinced themselves they could give a teenager like Nina a good home. A good start in life. Make a difference with her. They were good people."

Grant had a very bad feeling about this story. "What happened?" he asked reluctantly.

"Nina had only been in their home a month or so when things started missing—jewelry, trinkets, even some money that had been left lying around."

"So they blamed Nina?"

Trent shrugged. "It was a logical conclusion. The only other person who lived in the house was their housekeeper, and she'd been with them for years.

They'd never had any trouble until Nina came along. But they were still willing to give her a chance.''

"And?"

"She was caught red-handed taking money out of the man's wallet. Several hundred dollars. When she refused to own up to her mistakes, refused to change her ways, they felt they had no recourse but to take her back to the orphanage.''

Grant got up and paced to the window, staring out. "It was their word against Nina's, then.''

"Yes, but why would they lie, Grant? They wanted to adopt her. They took her into their home on good faith, but Nina turned against them. She lied, she stole, she proved over and over that she was out to get what she could no matter who she hurt. And unfortunately that behavior was repeated with my brother. And now with your family.''

It was a long time before Grant said anything. He couldn't reconcile the Nina he knew with the mercenary young girl Trent had just described. Something was wrong here. Something just didn't fit.

He turned back to Trent. "Why were she and Garrett getting a divorce?''

"Because the marriage had been a big mistake. Garrett finally realized that.''

"So you're saying the divorce was all his idea? Did he know Nina was pregnant?''

Trent shook his head. "No. She dropped that little bombshell a few days after the funeral, when she found out she wasn't getting any of Garrett's money.'' He paused, tracing the pattern on his boot with his fingertip. "Makes you wonder, doesn't it? They were in the middle of a bitter divorce, and yet they were still sleeping together? What kind of woman would do that?"

Grant tried to tamp down his sudden anger. His first impulse was to come to Nina's defense even as he told himself Trent had no reason to lie. "They could have tried to reconcile. That would explain the timing of her pregnancy."

Trent laughed bitterly. "There was no way Garrett would have tried to reconcile with her. He couldn't wait to get out of that marriage."

"So what are you saying?" Grant demanded. "Someone else fathered Nina's baby?" The words left a bad taste in his mouth.

Trent raised a brow. "I'm saying a little more than that, buddy. I'm saying I don't think Nina was ever pregnant."

Grant stared at him in shock. *"What?"*

"Think about it. According to the police, no one knew she was pregnant."

"She said she told you."

Trent's expression darkened. "Oh, she did tell me, but I saw right through her." He put both feet on the floor and sat forward in his chair suddenly. "Look, very few people know about this, but I'm pretty sure Garrett told Nina. Garrett's money—and mine, for that matter—was tied up in a trust fund established by our grandparents. Neither of us could touch the principal until we turned thirty. I received mine last year, but Garrett still had two more years to go. The trust stipulated that if either of us was to die before our thirtieth birthday, the money would then revert to the deceased's children, if he had any. The *children,* mind you, not the spouse. I think Nina was well aware of that clause."

Grant stared at him incredulously. "You think Nina faked a pregnancy in order to try and claim Garrett's trust fund? Why would she think she could get away with something like that?"

"Oh, she's gotten away with plenty in her life, believe me." Trent sat back in his chair. "I think she faked a pregnancy until she could get her hands on a baby."

"Jesus." Grant turned back to the window, his mind reeling in confusion. What the hell was Trent trying to do? None of this made any sense. "This is crazy," he said. "Someone did know about Nina's pregnancy. Her doctor. The police talked to him."

Trent laughed. "Oh, come on, Grant. You're not that naive. Doctors can be bought. She could have paid him to lie for her, to set up phony medical records, the whole bit. It's not impossible."

His words hit Grant like a physical blow. Hadn't Nina said the same thing about Vanessa's doctor? Nina had been so quick to come up with that theory, but still—

He turned back to Trent. "What about the hospital fire?"

"Nina could have set it herself, knowing that in all the confusion, no one would be able to confirm or deny her claim that she'd had a baby that night. All the records were destroyed."

Grant remembered what Farrell had told him, that the doctor who'd delivered Nina's baby was now in drug rehabilitation. He didn't even remember the fire, let alone delivering a baby that night. The one woman who did remember Nina was now dead. But that fact seemed to confirm Nina's story, didn't it?

That someone was out to stop her from finding the truth?

"You see, the fire covered her tracks," Trent explained. "And bought her some time. I have to admit, her plan worked brilliantly. Look at you." He paused, studying Grant. "I can tell by looking at you that she's already got you halfway convinced her story is true."

Grant didn't bother to deny it. "All right, let's just say I've bought into everything you've told me so far. Nina needed a baby in order to collect Garrett's trust. She started a fire at the hospital, burned all the records, then claimed she'd had Garrett's baby that night. But if she'd gone to all that trouble, why wouldn't she just have taken a baby during the uproar? Why would she claim Vanessa had stolen her baby?"

Trent smiled. "You haven't figured that out yet? Vanessa wasn't a stranger to Nina. She had a very good reason for wanting to get back at your sister."

If Grant had thought himself immune to any more shock, he was wrong. He walked over and sat behind his desk. "You're saying Vanessa and Nina know each other?"

"Not personally. But they know of each other."

"How?"

Trent hesitated, as if unsure where to begin. Finally he said, "While you were in Venezuela, Garrett and Vanessa became friends. More than friends, really. They became…close."

Grant glanced at him sharply. "How close?"

"Garrett told me they were serious, and that he wanted to marry her."

"So what happened?"

Trent shrugged. "I guess Vanessa wasn't quite as serious as Garrett. She broke off the relationship, and a few months later, announced her engagement to Clayton. Garrett was devastated."

Grant frowned, trying to digest everything Trent had told him. "Edwina didn't say a word about any of this when I talked to her a few days ago."

"She didn't know. Garrett didn't talk much about his private life, at least not to Mother. Anyway, after Clayton and Vanessa were married, Nina came along and Garrett was on the rebound. That's why he married her so quickly, without knowing anything about her background."

"You think Nina knew about Garrett and Vanessa's relationship?"

"I'm positive. Garrett told her, and she became jealous of Vanessa. Unreasonably so. I think she desperately wanted to get back at Vanessa."

Grant was still having a hard time reconciling the woman he knew with the picture Trent had so vividly painted. It was almost as if they were talking about two different people—Nina, and some woman Grant had never met. That he wouldn't want to meet. He scrubbed his face with his hands. "So what you've concluded is that Nina planned all along to claim her baby had been stolen, and she chose Vanessa as her target out of revenge?"

Trent drew a breath and released it. "I know it sounds far-fetched, but after I tell you the rest, I think you'll have to agree it all fits. Shortly before he died, Garrett confided to me that he and Vanessa had a one-night stand after they were both married. It was a mistake and they both regretted it, but…" He trailed off, studying Grant for a moment as if to gauge his reaction. "Vanessa thought she was pregnant."

Grant stared at him, stunned. "She said Garrett was the father?"

"She wasn't sure."

Grant couldn't believe what he was hearing. And yet as he sat there, shocked by what Trent was telling him, a memory came rushing back to him. *Tell me why you're so afraid of a DNA test,* he'd asked Vanessa.

He remembered her answer distinctly. *Because Clayton isn't John David's father.*

On the heels of the memory came another, this time of Nina. *Then how do you explain the fact that the baby looks exactly like my dead husband?*

Was it possible that Garrett Fairchild was John David's father? Was that why Nina thought the baby was hers?

Grant couldn't believe for a minute that the disappearance of Nina's baby was a hoax. He'd seen the pain and torment in her eyes. No one was that good of an actress. Unless…

God.

He closed his eyes for a moment.

No one was that good of an actress unless she really believed it was true. Unless she was so unbalanced the fabrication had become real to her.

But Nina wasn't unbalanced. Grant couldn't have been that wrong about her. He *knew* her, damn it. It didn't matter that they'd only met a few days ago. He knew her. He knew the kind of woman she was. The kind of woman he'd fallen in love with.

He drew a hand through his hair. "I don't believe any of this," he told Trent. "I don't believe Nina's the person you've described. I realize you and your family had problems with her, but I've spent time with her. I know her. I've..." He trailed off at Trent's knowing smile.

"You've come to care for her, right?" Trent shook his head. "Don't you see? She has that way about her. She makes you want to help her, to believe in her, but, Grant, you can't think this is all some strange coincidence. I mean, my brother's widow claiming that your sister stole her baby? Come on. This is no coincidence. This is all a part of Nina's carefully laid scheme. And you've unknowingly become her pawn."

THE DAY HAD GROWN CHILLY. Nina wrapped her sweater more tightly around her as she watched the mothers and their children playing in the park. The sound of laughter filled the air but didn't seem to touch the darkness inside her heart.

Someone had set fire to her office. Someone had killed Ruthanne Keller. Someone had made Sergeant Farrell doubt her story. Someone had deliberately set out to destroy her.

It sounded bizarre, but Nina knew it was true. Someone was out to destroy her credibility, to remove any trace of evidence that proved she'd had a baby. Of course, a medical examination could confirm she'd given birth, but not how long ago. Such a test wouldn't substantiate anything really, because by then, Nina would already look so incompetent, so *crazy* no one would care. No one would ever believe her.

The shadows in the park lengthened, and she shivered. The mothers began to pack up their strollers and gather their children to leave. In another half hour or so, Nina would be all alone in the park. Twilight would fall, and the weather would grow colder. But the prospect of returning to her empty house, now reeking of smoke, was even more bleak.

Nina wasn't sure how long she'd been sitting there. She'd left her house hours ago, after conferring with her insurance adjuster and wandering through the burned-out rubble. There was nothing to be salvaged, so she'd simply walked away. The cleanup would begin tomorrow by professionals, Nina would get back to work using the computer in her bedroom, and the world would continue to turn. But nothing would be the same.

Because she now realized exactly what she was up against. She'd known Vanessa Baldwin's family was powerful, but she'd had no idea how ruthless they were, or how far they were willing to go to stop her.

And at the center of it all was Grant. Nina closed her eyes, not wanting to believe the thoughts rushing through her head. He'd been with her last night when Ruthanne Keller had been killed. Nina wanted to believe that put him in the clear, but she couldn't forget the phone call he'd made earlier. The fire last night only deepened her feeling of dread. Grant knew where her office was. She'd told him once before that it was located in the back of her house.

"That's not proof," she whispered. Anyone could have found her office by simply walking around her house and looking in the windows. And Grant *had* been with her when Ruthanne was killed. Why couldn't she trust her instincts about him? Why couldn't she let herself believe that he was exactly the man he seemed to be, a man of honor and integrity, a man who would never be involved in keeping Nina from her son?

She had always suspected that Vanessa had an accomplice, someone who had helped her stage a pregnancy and buy off Dr. Mapleton, someone who had helped her start the hospital fire and kidnap Nina's son. These recent developments seemed to prove that. Vanessa hadn't been in any shape last evening to run down poor Ruthanne or to start the fire in Nina's office. Someone else had done that—the accomplice who seemed willing to do whatever it took to keep the truth from coming out.

So who was this accomplice? Vanessa's husband? Her father? Her brother?

Or, as Nina had always suspected, was Trent Fairchild involved in all this? His only connection to Vanessa appeared to be his friendship with Grant, but could there be more to their relationship than that?

Restless, Nina got up and began to walk. One thing she now knew for certain. The situation had become very dangerous, and she wanted more than ever to remove her son from that household. Who knew what might happen if either Vanessa or her accomplice was cornered? Nina would do anything, *anything* to protect her son.

And suddenly, with a clarity that was almost startling, she knew exactly what she had to do.

NINA PARKED HER CAR down the street from the Baldwin mansion and watched the house for signs of life. The estate was well lighted both inside and out. She had no way of knowing if Clayton was home, but she hoped he was still at the hospital with Vanessa. However, the house would not be empty in any case. The housekeeper would almost certainly be home, as well as the nanny. And if the nanny was there, that meant the baby was, too.

Nina took a deep breath, willing her heart to slow. It had been racing like mad ever since she'd first decided to come here, to put her daring plan into action.

Hearing a car, she jumped and glanced over her shoulder, almost expecting to see a police car pull up behind her. But the headlights turned down another street, and Nina released a long breath.

She couldn't stay here for long. River Oaks was a well-patrolled neighborhood. If the police didn't show up soon, the security guards would. She had to act quickly, but there was one major hitch to her plan. She wasn't sure how to gain entrance to the house without being detected.

Getting out of her car, Nina closed the door quietly and walked down the street, trying to appear as if she were a resident out for an evening stroll. When she drew even with the Baldwin home, she glanced over her shoulder, then darted into the thick shrubbery lining the driveway.

Trying to avoid the security lights, Nina hurried around to the back of the house. The backyard was heavily landscaped, making it easy to keep out of sight. But nearer the house, the foliage cleared, and Nina saw that the pool lights were on, illuminating the patio area.

She gazed up, wondering if she could pinpoint the window of the nursery. There was certainly no way to scale the wall, and for a moment, Nina wondered if the best thing to do was to go back around the house and ring the front doorbell. When the door was answered, she could push her way inside, run upstairs and grab the baby before anyone could stop her. She could be gone before the police ever arrived.

And then what? She and the baby would disappear forever. Nina would somehow have to get fake identification, another job, find them a place to live. She would be constantly looking over her shoulder, worrying when the police would arrive to take her son away from her again.

If she entered that house, she would never be free, and neither would her son. Did she have a right to force him into that kind of life?

Nina had tried to do the right thing. She'd gone to the police for help, but Sergeant Farrell refused to believe her. What else could she do? Why should she play by the rules when Vanessa Baldwin didn't have to?

Because I'm not like her.

Nina put trembling hands to her face as she stared up at the mansion. She wasn't like the Baldwins or the Chamberses or the Fairchilds. She had never considered herself above the law, but that was exactly what she was doing now.

She had to protect her son at any cost, but this wasn't the way to do it. If she was sent to jail for the rest of her life, what would happen to her baby then?

Her decision made, Nina turned to retrace her steps, but before she could move, a light caught her in the face, blinding her.

A man's voice said, "Don't move. I've got a gun on you."

Dimly Nina could see the shape of a man behind

the light. She put up a hand to shade her face, but the voice barked, "I said, don't move."

When Nina froze, the man called out, "Over here, Danny. It's her. The one they told us about. Better call Mr. Baldwin and find out what he wants us to do with her."

Chapter Thirteen

The moment Grant came out of the house, he saw Nina. She looked like a deer trapped in a headlight. His first emotion was one of relief, followed closely by anger. What was she doing here? And where the hell had she been while he'd been going out of his mind with worry?

"Look," she said to the guard. Her voice was shaky with fear. "This is all a mistake. I can explain everything."

"Save the explanations for Mr. Baldwin," the guard told her.

He reached for Nina's arm, and Grant called out, "What's going on here?"

The guard immediately whirled and caught Grant in the flashlight's beam. Grant put up a hand to shield his eyes. "Get that damn light out of my face."

The beam went out instantly. "Sorry, Mr. Chambers. I didn't know it was you."

The pool lights cast a soft glow over the yard, illuminating Nina's frightened features. She glanced at Grant, then away, as if she couldn't quite meet his eyes. "What's going on here?" he asked again.

The guard motioned toward Nina. "I caught her

snooping around the house. She's the woman Mr. Baldwin warned us about. Danny's calling him now to see what he wants us to do with her.''

The second guard materialized from the landscaping, cellular phone in hand.

''Did you make that call?'' the first guard demanded.

''I was just about to when I saw Mr. Chambers,'' Danny explained. Both men turned to Grant expectantly.

''Don't bother,'' he said to Danny.

The first guard looked at him in surprise. ''But we have our orders. Mr. Baldwin was very specific. If this woman showed up anywhere near the premises, we're to alert him PDQ.''

''I realize that,'' Grant said. ''But my brother-in-law is spending the evening with my sister at the hospital. I don't think it would be a good idea to bother them with this incident. Not tonight. I don't want to worry my sister.''

The guard hesitated. ''I can understand that, but what do you think we should do? Call the police?''

Grant hesitated, studying Nina's face, searching for signs of guilt. For signs of the woman Trent Fairchild had described to him that morning. Could she really be that good of an actress?

She glanced at Grant almost defiantly, and anger surged through him. Anger at her. Anger at the situation. Anger because he didn't know whom or what to believe anymore.

Without taking his eyes off Nina, he said, ''I'll take care this.''

''But—''

''Don't worry,'' Grant told the wary guard. ''I'll

take full responsibility. You two go on about your business, and I'll handle the situation here.''

The guard named Danny turned immediately to follow Grant's orders, but the first guard seemed a little less certain. After a slight hesitation, he left without arguing. When the two men had disappeared into the shadows, Grant turned back to Nina.

''What the hell are you doing here?'' He grasped her shoulders. ''Do you have any idea how worried I've been?''

She blinked up at him, as if his words didn't quite register. ''Why?''

''Why?'' Grant tried to get a grip on his emotions. Now that they were alone, his anger began to fade. He remembered how he'd felt earlier when he'd gone by her house and had seen the burned-out room. He hadn't known what had happened to her, but he'd thought the worst. An overwhelming relief came over him now, and he had to fight the urge to pull her into his arms and hold her close. It didn't seem to matter that she had been caught at his sister's house when she'd promised to stay away. All he cared about at the moment was that she was safe.

''I went by your house and saw there'd been a fire. None of your neighbors knew anything about it. No one knew what had happened or where you'd gone to. I called the fire department, the police, every hospital in the city looking for you. When I couldn't find you—'' He broke off when he saw the look in Nina's eyes.

''You were worried about me?''

''Of course I was worried. What did you expect?''

She seemed very unsure of herself. ''It's just that...''

For the first time, Grant understood what Nina's life must have been like, how different it had been from his. Even though he didn't always get along with his family, he couldn't imagine what it would be like without them.

He stared down at Nina, at the uncertainty in her eyes, the pride and dignity in her bearing, and the emotion that surged through him wasn't pity, but admiration.

She has a way about her. She makes you want to help her.

Grant swore under his breath, wishing to hell he'd never had that conversation with Trent Fairchild. But the conversation *had* taken place, questions had been raised and, like it or not, he would have to confront Nina with Trent's allegations.

"How did you know to look for me here?" she asked.

Grant shrugged. "I didn't. It was a last resort, but I realize now this is the first place I should have thought to look. You came here to take John David, didn't you?"

His blunt accusation seemed to startle her. Grant could have sworn she was about to deny it, but then, after a tense pause, she surprised him by admitting it. "Can you blame me? After everything that's happened, I'm afraid for him. A woman's been killed, Grant. You can't ignore that."

"I'm not. But kidnapping isn't the answer."

"He's my son."

"Not in the eyes of the law." He took her shoulders, forcing her to look up at him. "Are you really willing to risk spending the rest of your life in jail?"

Her eyes filled. "I would do a lot more than that for my son."

Her tears were very nearly Grant's undoing. "This isn't the answer, Nina," he said softly.

She drew a long breath. "I know that. It didn't take me long to figure out that even if I did find a way into the house and managed to take the baby without anyone seeing me, we'd always be on the run. We'd always be trying to stay one step ahead of the law. I didn't want that for my son." She paused, her eyes pleading for understanding. "I just want to see him again. I just want to hold him in my arms. Grant, please—"

"Don't ask that of me now."

"But you promised—"

"I know I promised," he said in anguish. His hands dropped from her arms, and he took a step back from her. "I know I promised," he said more quietly. "But now is not the time. The guards saw you here, and you can be sure they'll report to Clayton. Maybe not tonight, but soon. We can't give them any more ammunition against you. We have to get you out of here. I'll drive you home."

"You don't have to drive me. My car is parked down the street."

"Then I'll follow you." His voice hardened. "We've got a lot to talk about, Nina. A lot of things we have to get straight."

IN LESS THAN TWENTY minutes, Nina pulled into her driveway while Grant parked at the curb in front of her house. She got out and waited for him on the sidewalk, then together they climbed the porch steps and she unlocked her front door.

The stale scent of smoke clung to the air. "Sorry about the smell," Nina said, removing her jacket.

Grant did the same, and she hung both of their coats on a rack near the front door. "I expected it to be worse, judging by the damage. Did you lose anything valuable?"

Nina looked at him. "That room was my office. My computer was destroyed, along with all my files and records."

"I'm sorry." He followed her into the living room, and she motioned to the sofa. They both sat, and Grant turned to her. "Do you have any idea how the fire started?"

"One of the firemen thinks it may have been deliberately set."

Grant lifted a brow. "Why does he think that? Did he find something suspicious?"

Was it Nina's imagination, or was his tone a little more anxious than was necessary? "Not yet. But we'll know more when the arson investigators finish their report."

Grant sat back against the sofa. "My God," he said. "I had no idea."

"No idea of what?" she asked sharply.

He met her gaze. "Vanessa was in the hospital last night. She couldn't have had anything to do with the fire. Or with Ruthanne Keller's death."

Nina wanted to argue that Vanessa could very well have had an accomplice, but what would be the point? She had her opinion, and Grant had his.

"What was it you wanted to talk to me about?" she asked him.

"I'd like to know more about the adoption you

told me about last night. The one that didn't go through.''

Nina felt an odd queasiness in her stomach. Why did he want to know about that? ''It happened a long time ago. What does it matter now?''

His gaze met hers once more. ''It matters, Nina.''

''I...see.'' She did see. The revelation came swiftly. ''So you've been talking to Trent again.''

''He came to my office today. He made some pretty serious allegations.''

''Yes,'' she said bitterly. ''He's always been very good at that.'' Nina told herself she was foolish to feel so betrayed, but she couldn't help it. She got up and walked to the window, staring out. ''The couple's names were John and Marlene Webster. They were very wealthy and very dignified, and from the first moment I saw them, I was terrified of them.''

''Why?''

She heard the surprise in his voice and turned to face him briefly. ''Because the life they were offering me was so far removed from anything I'd ever known. I didn't want to go home with them, but, of course, I didn't have a choice. The sisters tried to make it easier for me by reminding me of all the wonderful opportunities the Websters could give me.''

''So what happened?''

She sensed rather than saw Grant get up and move toward her. Nina tensed, but he kept his distance. She wasn't sure whether to be relieved or heartbroken. There seemed to be such a chasm between them tonight.

''As I told you last night, they gave me beautiful clothes, enrolled me in a very exclusive private school, paraded me in front of their friends and business associates to display their generosity.''

''And?''

Nina folded her arms around her middle. ''And then one day Mr. Webster came on to me.''

She sensed Grant's shock, glanced at him to see his face darken in anger. ''What happened, Nina?''

''I was alone one day. Mrs. Webster was still at some meeting, and Mr. Webster came home early. He barged into my room without knocking and tried to...touch me.''

Grant took her arm. ''Did he hurt you?''

Nina shook her head. ''No. It wasn't anything like that. But when I...wouldn't cooperate and threatened to tell Mrs. Webster—Mother, as she'd instructed me to call her—he said that I'd be sorry if I ever told anyone. He said that he'd already informed his wife that some of their things were missing—cash, jewelry, things that like. If I didn't keep my mouth shut, he'd see to it that the police would come to the house and take me off to jail.''

''Nice guy,'' Grant muttered. ''What did you do?''

''The only thing I could do,'' Nina said. ''I kept my mouth shut. The next day, Mrs. Webster confronted me. She said her husband had told her about catching me taking money—several hundred dollars—from his wallet, and that they felt they had no recourse but to return me to the convent where I could get the strict moral guidance I obviously needed. So I went back to the orphanage and stayed until I finished high school.'' Nina turned to Grant. ''That's it. That's what you wanted to know. Whether you believe me or not is up to you.''

''I believe you,'' he said quietly.

Nina wanted to take comfort in his words, but she knew they weren't done yet. Not by a long shot. Trent Fairchild had done a real number on her when she'd been married to his brother, and Nina had no doubt that he'd done the same today, with Grant.

She glanced at him. "What else did you want to know?"

Grant paused ever so briefly. For the first time that night, he looked uncertain. "Before all this started, everything with John David, did you know Vanessa?"

Nina stared at him in shock. She hadn't expected this. "Of course I didn't. I never met her before in my life until...well, until I met her in the park as Karen Smith."

Grant let that one pass. "Garrett never mentioned her to you?"

Nina shook her head. "No. Why?"

He turned away, walking back to the sofa, but he didn't sit down. Instead he faced her from a distance. For some reason, the action seemed ominous to Nina.

"Trent said that you did know her."

"He's lying."

"Why would he do that?"

"Because he hates me," Nina said, her stomach trembling inside. What if she couldn't make him believe her? "Trent and his mother have always blamed me for Garrett's death. He would do anything to destroy me. I've often wondered if he didn't have something to do with Dustin's disappearance."

"That's a pretty serious allegation of your own," Grant said. "I've known Trent Fairchild for years."

"I see your dilemma," Nina said angrily. "Who

are you to believe, a lifelong friend or a woman whom you've known for less than a week?''

Grant's gaze was piercing. ''There's no contest as far as I'm concerned.''

Nina's heart hammered against her chest as he crossed the room toward her. ''I don't think Trent's lying,'' he said. ''But I do think he's mistaken.''

''But just moments ago, you had doubts about *me,*'' she said. ''All those questions—''

''I wanted to hear your side. And now that I have, I believe you.''

Nina's eyes welled with tears. She wanted to walk into his arms and remain there forever. It seemed to her the cruelest of fates that she and Grant had been pitted against each other in a drama few people could ever imagine. And in the middle of it all was a tiny little boy who had no idea what was going on.

''What do we do now?'' she whispered.

Grant's jaw tightened as he stared down at her. ''I'm going to get to the bottom of all this. I don't know how or when, but I promise you, the truth will come out. You have to trust me on that.''

He said it almost in challenge. The gauntlet had been tossed before her. Grant had chosen to believe her over a friend he had known for years. Could she do the same for him? Could she throw away a lifetime of distrust and put her faith in Grant?

''I...do trust you,'' she said hesitantly. ''I don't know why, but I do.''

He smiled down at her. ''I think you do know why.''

He took a step toward her, and for one wild moment, Nina thought that he would take her in his arms and kiss her like he had last evening on the beach. Her stomach fluttered with excitement as she realized how much she wanted him to do just that.

But instead he stood very close, not touching her at all, and yet the way he looked at her was more intimate than any kiss or caress could ever be.

"People in love believe in one another. They trust each other, Nina. It's the most sacred of all trusts."

His words took her breath away. "In…love?"

He still didn't touch her, but their gazes locked. Nina didn't dare look away. "Can you deny it?"

She couldn't. God help her, she couldn't.

"But how can we be? With everything…" She made a helpless gesture with her hand. Grant captured her hand, entwining her fingers with his.

"It's simple for me. Loving you is like breathing."

Nina closed her eyes. "But it isn't simple, Grant. You and I both know the whole situation is impossible."

"No, it's not." He pressed a fingertip to her lips, silencing her protests. "I've made a decision. I've been thinking about what we discussed yesterday in Galveston."

Nina's heart tripped inside her. "The DNA test, you mean?"

He nodded, but his eyes clouded briefly. "I've decided to do it. I've already talked to a lab. We can have the results back in about a week."

Nina couldn't believe what she was hearing. In a week, she could have proof that the baby known as John David Baldwin was, in fact, Dustin Fairchild, her son. Her elation was tempered only by the glimmer of emotion in Grant's eyes. He would help, but at what cost?

Nina didn't know what to say. She squeezed his hand. "I can't believe you're willing to do this for me."

His gazed darkened as he stared down at her. "I'd do a lot more than that for you." But before Nina had time to savor his words, he added, "If the test proves conclusively that you aren't John David's mother, then Vanessa never has to know about this."

"And if the test proves I am his mother?"

Grant glanced away. "We'll deal with it."

Their hands were still linked, and Nina drew his fingers to her cheek. "I don't know what to say. How to thank you. I know what this must be costing you."

"I'm not sure you do. I've always protected Vanessa, always made sure no harm came to her. The thought of betraying her, especially now when she's so sick—" He broke off, gazing down at her. "But what I'm experiencing is nothing compared to what you've been through. I want this nightmare to end for you, Nina. I'll do anything to make that happen."

Without thinking of the consequences, without holding herself back, Nina walked into Grant's arms. She laid her head against his chest, hearing the comforting thud of his heart and thinking that at last, after all the years of loneliness, she'd finally found true love.

Her relationship with Garrett had been nothing like this. He had willingly believed lies about her, had turned his back on her, and had, in the end, chosen his family over her. But Grant…Grant had so much more to lose, and yet he was willing to risk it all for her.

She tilted her face up to his. He stroked her cheek, his eyes deep and dark with emotion. When he lowered his head to hers, Nina welcomed him with every fiber of her being. Her lips parted, her tongue touched his and desire, quick and hot, spiraled through her.

He pulled her close, his hands stroking her back, her hips, the sides of her breasts. Everywhere he touched, Nina tingled with excitement. Her whole body quivered with anticipation. She wanted him, she realized, as she had never wanted any man before.

Nina wasn't sure how they ended up on the sofa, but suddenly Grant was lying over her, his lips trailing kisses along her jawbone, finding the tender, erotic pulse point in her throat. She arched her body into his, wrapping her arms around him, wanting everything his dark eyes seemed to promise.

It was the ringing of the telephone that finally drew them apart. Grant lifted himself up from her. "You'd better get that," he said, his breathing ragged.

Nina, self-conscious now that reality had intruded, sat up and adjusted her clothes as she reached for the phone. When she recognized Sergeant Farrell's voice, she tensed. "Do you have news, Sergeant?"

He paused. "Yes."

Something in his tone made Nina's heart almost stop. "What is it? What's happened?"

Grant turned his head to stare at her.

"I'm afraid this may come as a shock to you, Nina," Farrell said.

Nina's first thought was that something had happened to her baby. They'd found him, but something was wrong.

"Dear God." Her hands shook so badly, the phone

slipped loose. Nina grabbed for it, but couldn't seem to make her fingers work. The receiver thudded against the floor.

"Nina, are you all right?" Grant asked. When she didn't answer, he reached over and retrieved the phone, lifting it to his ear. "Sergeant Farrell? Grant Chambers. I gather you have some bad news for Nina."

Nina sat helplessly watching Grant's face as he listened to Farrell. She knew with certainty that something had happened to her baby, and she couldn't stand to hear it.

In a moment or two, Grant hung up the phone and turned to Nina. "It's not what you think. It wasn't about the baby."

It took a moment for his words to register. Nina stared at him blankly. "Not about the baby?"

"That wasn't why Sergeant Farrell called."

Relief washed over her as his words finally sank in. "It wasn't about my baby?"

Grant shook his head. It occurred to Nina that while he still sat next to her, he hadn't made a move to touch her. To comfort her. And his expression was more grim that she had ever seen it.

Whatever momentary joy Nina experienced fled. "What is it?"

Grant studied her for a moment, then rose to his feet. Nina suddenly felt tiny and insignificant gazing up at him.

"We're to meet Sergeant Farrell in his office tomorrow afternoon. He has someone he wants us to talk to."

Nina frowned. "Who?"

"Karen Smith. It seems she's flying in from California tonight."

Chapter Fourteen

By five o'clock the next day, Grant and Nina were pulling into the parking lot adjacent to the police station in Galveston. Nina hadn't slept a wink the night before, nor had she been able to get any rest that day. Her thoughts churned with confusion. How could she be meeting with Karen Smith in Sergeant Farrell's office today if Karen Smith and Vanessa Baldwin were the same person? Vanessa was in the hospital. Her condition had improved but was still very serious. There was no way she could be present at this meeting.

Nina clasped her hands in her lap as she stared out the window. Could she have been mistaken about everything?

And what about Grant? How would this change things between them? Last night he'd believed in her, trusted her, but now—how could he, when everything she'd told him, everything she'd sworn to hinged on the woman inside Farrell's office?

They didn't speak as they got out of the car and walked across the parking lot to the building. Sergeant Farrell was waiting for them in the lobby. He shook hands with Grant and nodded to Nina. His expression seemed guarded and wary.

"She's waiting in my office," he said.

"How do you know she's really Karen Smith?" Nina asked, not daring to look at Grant's face. "Maybe she's just claiming to be. Maybe someone hired her to throw us off track."

"I've done some checking," Farrell said. "Her story seems to hold up."

"*Seems* to?" Nina asked.

Grant surprised Nina by asking, "If she is Karen Smith, why did she wait until now to come forward?"

Nina glanced at him gratefully, but his eyes were on Farrell.

The detective shrugged. "She said that when she and her husband moved to California, she lost all contact with friends and acquaintances in Houston. Then a couple of days ago, she happened to see a magazine article about missing children. Nina's and Dustin's names were mentioned, and according to Ms. Smith, she was horrified to see her own name listed as a possible suspect in the case. She contacted my office immediately."

"So why were the police never able to find her until now?" Grant asked.

"Karen Smith is a common name, and we had nothing else to go on except a description. No address, no place of employment, nothing. We didn't even know her husband's name. The computer searches turned up dozens of Karen Smiths, but none of them panned out." Nina thought he sounded a little on the defensive side, but she couldn't really blame him. He'd been searching for this woman for six months, and then one day, out of the blue, she called *him*.

"Why don't we save the questions for later," he said. "Let's get the meeting over with."

Nina grew even more nervous as she followed Farrell down the corridor to his office. The door was ajar, and she could see a dark-haired woman inside. When the woman shifted slightly, Nina saw that she was wearing glasses.

As Farrell stepped into the office, the woman turned to face the door. When she saw Nina, she rose from her seat.

Nina's heart almost stopped. She couldn't move. For an eternity, she stood staring at the dark-haired woman wearing glasses. The woman who called herself Karen Smith. The woman whose eyes lit in recognition the moment she saw Nina.

Behind her, Grant took her elbow, nudging her inside the office. Then he closed the door behind them.

The woman rushed forward and enveloped Nina in a hug. Her perfume smelled eerily familiar. Nina stepped back from the woman's embrace and stared at her.

"My God, what you've been through!" the woman cried. "I had no idea. You can't imagine what a shock it was to see your name in that article and to realize that you were the same Nina I'd known. And then to see my own name—" She turned to Farrell. "I can't believe I've been a suspect this whole time. I didn't even know about any of this." She faced Nina again. "I'm so sorry, Nina. I had no idea any of this had happened."

Nina felt as if she were trapped in some sort of

bizarre nightmare. Nothing seemed real. Her mind was numb with shock. "Who are you?" she whispered. "Why are you doing this to me?"

Confusion clouded the woman's eyes. Her glance went to Grant standing behind Nina, then back to Nina. "I don't understand. Don't you remember me? We were so close. All those long talks we had in the park. All the secrets we shared. You can't have forgotten me."

Nina took a step back from the woman and felt Grant's comforting hand on her back. *Easy now,* he seemed to be saying.

But hysteria welled inside Nina. "You're not *her*. You're not Karen Smith. Who sent you here? Who's paying you to lie?"

The woman looked genuinely hurt. "Nina, it *is* me. I *am* Karen." She bit her lip, as if unsure what else to say, then her face suddenly brightened. "Look, I can prove it to you. I remember all the things you told me. You were raised in an orphanage in San Antonio. The nuns found you outside the convent's gates. You never knew who your real parents were. After you left the convent, you lived alone until you met and married a man named Garrett Fairchild. He was killed before learning you were pregnant." She stopped and spread her hands in supplication. "There. How could I know all that if you hadn't told me?"

"Because someone else told you," Nina accused. "Someone coached you."

"No one coached me. I *am* Karen. I don't know why you're doing this—" The woman broke off suddenly, as if a revelation had just occurred to her. Her eyes filled with pity.

Something snapped inside Nina at that look. She turned and placed her hands on Farrell's desk, leaning toward him in urgency. "Don't you see what she's doing? Someone paid her to come here. They want to discredit me even more than they already have. Make me seem delusional. You can't let them get away with this."

"Calm down, Nina," Farrell advised.

"Calm down!" Nina whirled to face Grant. "She's lying, Grant. You have to believe me."

The look on his face told her he didn't know what to believe. Fear exploded inside Nina. If Grant didn't believe her, no one would. He was her only hope.

The dark-haired woman shook her head sadly. "I can only imagine what she's been through. Losing her baby like that—"

"She's lying!" Nina cried. "I can't believe you can't see through her."

"Nina—"

Grant reached out for her, but she shook off his hand. She flung open the door and fled the office, aware of the curious eyes as she ran down the corridor to the lobby. Outside, she paused on the steps in front of the station, gulping air. Her heart flailed against her chest. She put her hands to her face, not knowing where to go or whom to turn to.

Grant came out of the station behind her. Nina started to walk away from him, but he caught up with her and took her arm. "You're going the wrong way," he said. "The car's over here."

She let him lead her to the car. "She was lying, Grant. That woman was not Karen Smith. At least, not the Karen Smith I knew."

"Then Farrell will find out the truth about her," Grant said, his expression grave.

"But what if he doesn't? What if he just accepts her word for it?"

"He's a professional, Nina. We have to trust him to do his job."

"But I don't trust him anymore." Nina stared up at Grant, willing his support. "Someone's told him lies about me. He's turned against me. Can't you see that?"

Grant's mouth tightened almost imperceptibly. "Then we'll hire a private investigator to check her out."

His words helped calm Nina for a moment. She leaned against his car, her gaze searching his face. "Do you believe me?"

He seemed at a loss. "This whole thing is so bizarre. I don't know what the hell to think anymore."

"At least you're being honest," Nina said bitterly, although she couldn't help but remember what he'd told her last night, that people in love believed in one another, trusted each other. Where was that trust now? Where was his blind faith in her when she needed it the most?

Nina knew she was being unfair, but she couldn't help it. Grant had been her only hope, and now she felt him slipping away from her.

"I don't care who that woman is," she said angrily. "It doesn't change anything. John David is still my son. Someone paid her to lie."

"Nina—"

"But there's one thing they can't lie about. The fact that the baby looks exactly like Garrett."

Nina, staring up at Grant, saw his expression alter.

His eyes darkened with an emotion she didn't understand.

He took a deep breath and released it. "There's something you don't know."

Her heart sank at the look on his face. "What?"

He paused, as if unsure what to say. "Do you remember last night when I told you that Trent had said you and Vanessa knew each other?"

"I told you he was lying."

"I know. He also told me that Garrett and Vanessa had a brief affair while she was married to Clayton and Garrett was married to you."

Nina's mouth dropped open. "An affair? Garrett and…Vanessa? I don't believe it." What didn't she believe? That her husband had cheated on her, or that it had been with Vanessa?

"I don't know if it's true," Grant said. "I'm just telling you what he said. He also told me that when Vanessa got pregnant, she thought Garrett might be the father."

The air left Nina's lungs in a painful rush. For a moment, she couldn't breathe and panic engulfed her.

"No," she whispered.

Grant stared down at her. "You see what I'm getting at, don't you? If all this is true, then it would explain why Vanessa's baby looks like your dead husband."

THE TRIP HOME WAS SILENT, just as the earlier trip to Galveston had been. Nina's thoughts whirled with confusion. Garrett and Vanessa? Was it possible? Could they really have had an affair and Nina not know about it?

Of course they could, she thought angrily. It happened all the time. But what she couldn't believe was that Garrett had fathered Vanessa's baby.

Nina put trembling hands to her face. Why was this happening? Why was she only now finding out about her husband and another woman—Vanessa Baldwin, of all people? Why was some woman pretending to be Karen Smith? Who had sent her, and why?

There was only one explanation. Nina was being driven slowly and methodically insane. No one would believe her wild accusations after all this. Not even Grant.

She glanced at his profile, but he didn't turn to meet her gaze. He kept his eyes on the road, and the granite set of his jaw and chin told Nina more than she wanted to know.

When at last they reached Houston and Grant pulled into the parking area of an apartment complex, Nina asked in alarm, "Where are we?"

"I live here." Grant killed the engine and glanced at her. "I don't think you should be alone tonight."

Nina lifted a brow. "Why? Do you think I might go off the deep end? Do something drastic?"

Something flickered across his features. "The thought never crossed my mind. You're the strongest person I've ever known."

Before Nina could answer, or even digest what he'd said, he got out of the car and came around to help her out. He took her hand and didn't release it until they were inside his apartment, and he'd turned on the light.

Nina stared at the unfamiliar surroundings, feeling disoriented. The leather-and-brass furnishings were unmistakably masculine, and it hit Nina suddenly just exactly where she was. She was alone with Grant in his apartment, and no matter what kind of tension and strain they'd been under since Farrell had called about Karen Smith, Nina still couldn't deny her feelings.

She cleared her throat and turned away.

"Let me take your jacket," Grant said. He was careful to barely touch her while he helped remove her coat, then he tossed it to a chair with his.

An uncomfortable silence settled around them. Grant broke it by saying, "How about some dinner? I'll see what I can find in the kitchen."

Nina shook her head. "I'm not hungry."

"You have to eat. I'll bet you haven't had a decent meal in days."

Not since he'd taken her to Americas, Nina thought. Had that really only been a few days ago? In some ways, it seemed like a lifetime.

"I don't want anything. I'm just…tired." She sat down on the leather sofa, suddenly drained. Today's revelations had taken their toll.

"Why don't you stretch out on the bed, then?" Grant suggested. "Maybe you can get a little sleep. I left my number with Farrell. He'll call if there are any new developments."

Nina hesitated. Somehow sleeping in Grant's bed was taking their relationship a step further than she was ready to go. "The couch is fine. I'll just lay down for a few minutes here."

He reached down and took her hand, pulling her to her feet. "Don't be stubborn," he said. "The bed is a lot more comfortable."

Reluctantly Nina followed him into the bedroom,

glancing around curiously in spite of herself. The same masculine colors—navy, maroon and hunter green—had been carried through in here. Nina watched as he turned down the bed, adjusted the pillows, then waited while she removed her shoes and slipped between the sheets. He drew the covers over her and then reached to turn off the lamp. Suddenly Nina didn't want to be in darkness. She didn't want to be alone.

She reached for Grant's hand before he could touch the light switch. He stared down at her questioningly, but when she didn't say anything—*couldn't* say anything—he murmured, "I think I'll sit with you for a while. Do you mind?"

Nina smiled gratefully. "I'd like that."

He left the light on, then moved around to lie down on the other side of the bed. He didn't get under the covers, but instead stretched his legs on top of the bedspread and leaned back against the headboard.

Nina rolled over to face him. After a moment, she said, "That woman wasn't Karen Smith, Grant. You have to believe me."

He reached over to tuck an errant strand of hair behind her ear. The gesture was tender and protective, and made Nina want to cry. "I'll have her investigated myself, and I'll make damn sure Farrell does his job. I'll find out everything I can about her. I'm still on your side, Nina. That hasn't changed. But if that woman turns out to be who she says she is—"

Nina rolled to her back, staring at the ceiling. "She won't."

"But if she does, then a DNA test on John David won't be necessary."

Nina closed her eyes. "Because he won't be my son. That's what you believe anyway, isn't it? That he's Vanessa and Garrett's son?"

"There is that possibility, Nina."

She turned back to face him. "But if John David really is Vanessa's, then where is my son? Who took him? Is he all right? Is he even still alive?" Her voice cracked as the questions bubbled out of her. For the first time in a very long time, Nina felt on the verge of losing control. She blinked back tears, hardened her resolve, but the moment Grant drew her into his arms, her defenses melted.

She sobbed quietly against his chest, and he held her close, smoothing her hair with his hand, whispering to her that everything would be all right, that he would make sure of it.

No one had ever comforted Nina like this before. The nuns at the orphanage had always stressed to Nina and the other children the importance of self-reliance. So Nina had grown up, never needing anyone. Or so she'd told herself. But she needed Grant now. So much it frightened her.

After a bit, she drew away from him, wiping her face with her hands. "I'm sorry. I've never done that before."

"Maybe you should have." She heard the smile in his voice.

Nina sniffed. "I didn't think I could. There was never anyone around to pick up the pieces for me."

"Well, there is now." He thumbed away a stray tear.

Nina felt another onslaught of emotions at his words. "I don't know why you're here for me. After everything that's happened. With that woman claiming she's Karen Smith—''

He caught one of her hands in his. "I'm here no matter what happens. Can't you understand that?''

Nina drew a shaky breath. "Maybe I'm beginning to.''

She looked up at him then, and her heart almost stopped. Before she had time to catch her breath, he bent toward her, catching her lips in a soft, possessive kiss.

He pulled back, staring deeply into her eyes. "I'm sorry. I know this isn't the right time.''

"I think it may be the perfect time,'' she whispered. Weaving her fingers through his hair, she drew him toward her, pressing her lips against his until the kiss deepened and the moment heated.

With a low groan, Grant slid down in bed, drawing her even more tightly into his arms. But the bedspread was a frustrating barrier between them. Breaking away, he whipped the covers back until they were lying with their bodies so close, she couldn't tell the difference between her heartbeat and his.

This probably *wasn't* the right time, she thought fleetingly. Her emotions were too raw, but the right time might never come. Not for her and Grant. Was it wrong to want a few stolen moments of passion? Of love?

Grant rolled over her, propping himself on his elbows as he stared down at her. "I do love you,'' he said, as if sensing what she needed to hear. His hand whispered along the neckline of her sweater, sending a deep thrill of excitement down her backbone.

Nina shivered. "I love you, too. I don't understand it, but I do.''

She ran her hands down the front of his shirt, finding the buttons and undoing them. Grant reciprocated by pulling her sweater over her head and tossing it to the floor with his shirt.

Nina closed her eyes as thrill after thrill washed over her. The rest of their clothes would come next, and then they would be naked, completely exposed to one another. Grant would hold her and kiss her and touch her, until she would cry out in passion. He would make love to her, maybe more than once, until she would lie spent and sated beside him. As the images tumbled through her mind, the anticipation became almost unbearable.

Nina opened her eyes and found Grant staring down at her. He smiled a slow, knowing smile. "Some things are meant to be, Nina."

She drew him to her, whispering against his mouth, "Then show me."

THE RINGING of the telephone awakened Nina with a start. For a moment, she thought she was in her own bed, and then the memories flooded back. She turned over, searching for Grant, but the space beside her was empty.

The telephone rang again, and Nina sat up, looking around. The door to the bathroom was ajar, and she could hear the shower running inside. Should she answer the phone? she wondered. It could be Sergeant Farrell or the hospital calling about Vanessa. In either case, Grant would want to know.

But before Nina could reach for the phone, the answering machine came on and Grant's voice instructed the caller to leave a message after the beep.

Nina drew the covers around her as she listened.

A vaguely familiar voice said, "I just came from the hospital, Grant. The doctor said Vanessa's doing better, but I'm still worried about her. I know you are, too. We've had our problems in the past, but the one thing we've always agreed upon is that Vanessa has to be protected."

Nina realized the caller must be Grant's father. She glanced toward the bathroom, wondering if Grant would come out at any moment and catch her listening to his message. But the shower was still running, and Nina turned back to the phone.

"That woman concerns me," J.D. Chambers was saying. "We can't let these wild accusations of hers go on. Something has got to be done about her."

Nina's heart started to pound. What was he suggesting?

"Look, I don't know what your plan is to get rid of her, but you'd better speed it up. By the time Vanessa is released from the hospital, I want that woman out of our lives for good. I'm counting on you to take care of her, Grant. Don't let me down."

The machine recorded the disconnect, and then everything was silent except for the thunder of Nina's heart in her ears. She felt as if she were drowning, in over her head and nowhere to go but down.

I don't know what your plan is to get rid of her, but you'd better speed it up… I'm counting on you to take care of her, Grant.

Grant's plan suddenly became crystal clear to Nina. Get close to her. Find out her weaknesses. Use her emotions against her.

And she had played right into his hands. She had let him convince her to help her, when all along what he really wanted to do was stay one step ahead of her. Set her up to look as if she were going crazy. How could she have been so blind?

Nina found her clothes and slipped them on quickly. She glanced at the bathroom door, knowing that she should stay and confront Grant, make him tell her the truth about his plan, about John David, everything.

But with all that had happened that day, she was feeling too weak and vulnerable. She had to leave, gather her strength, and then, when the time was right, she would strike back.

She let herself out of Grant's apartment, shivering in the cold night air. She'd forgotten her jacket, but she wouldn't go back to get it. Besides, her house was only a few blocks away, and if she was lucky, she could get there and be safely inside before Grant ever realized she was missing.

She could sit down and plan her strategy, decide the best course of action to take to get back her son.

Nina took off walking down the street. Right now she wouldn't let herself think of what Grant's betrayal meant to her as a woman in love.

Think about Dustin, Nina ordered herself. *He's the only one who matters in all this.*

WHEN GRANT GOT OUT of the shower and dried off, his first instinct was to crawl back into bed with Nina and pick up where they'd left off earlier. He wanted her now more than ever, and had to resist the temptation to awaken her, to rekindle the incredible passion they'd shared.

But she was exhausted, both physically and emotionally, and he knew what she needed more than anything now was rest. She would need all her strength in the coming days.

Was the woman they'd met earlier in Farrell's office really Karen Smith? And if she wasn't, what did that mean? Had someone really hired her to lie?

The questions formed faster than Grant could find answers, but after tonight, he was more determined than ever to help Nina find her son. No matter where he was or who had taken him.

The first thing Grant saw when he walked into the bedroom was the empty bed. He glanced around. "Nina?" Crossing the room to the hallway, he called out louder. "Nina?"

Her clothes were gone. She must have left, but why? Had she awakened and had regrets about what they'd done?

He hated to think of her out on the street alone at this time of night. Drawing on his clothes, he picked up his car keys from the nightstand and turned to go find her when the phone rang. Thinking it might be her, he grabbed up the receiver.

"Nina?"

A pause. "Is this Mr. Chambers?"

"Yes." For the first time, Grant noticed the message light blinking. Someone must have called while he'd been in the shower.

The voice on the other end of the line said, "My name is Kaylin McDougal. I'm a nurse at the hospital. I work in the CCU. Your number was left as a contact in case of an emergency."

Grant's heart thudded against his chest. "Is it Vanessa?"

"Yes, sir. The doctor asked me to call you. He wants you to get here as quickly as possible."

Chapter Fifteen

Kaylin McDougal met Grant in the hallway outside Vanessa's room in the CCU. "The doctor's in with her now. He'll be out shortly to speak with you."

"What happened?" Grant asked. "She was doing so much better."

"We don't know. One of the nurses at the desk said your sister had a visitor a little while ago. Soon after he left, she became extremely agitated. The doctor's very worried about her."

"Who was the visitor?" Grant asked.

"I'm sorry, but I don't know."

Grant glanced at his sister's room. The blinds were drawn over the window so that no one could look in. "Did you call my father and her husband?"

"I couldn't reach either one of them. Your number was on the list, too. The doctor was adamant that someone from the family should be here."

Grant wondered if the woman had any idea how ominous she sounded. She excused herself and went back to work, and Grant waited for the doctor to come out of Vanessa's room. When he did a few minutes later, his expression was grave.

"Your sister's condition has taken a downward

turn, I'm afraid. Normally I wouldn't allow visitors under the circumstances, but she's asking to see you. I think you'd better go in, but keep in mind that it is imperative she remain calm."

"Of course."

After the doctor left, Grant opened the door and went in. Vanessa's eyes were closed, and he thought for a moment she was sleeping. He pulled up a chair beside her bed and sat down, taking her hand in his. Her skin felt cold and lifeless. It threw him for a moment, seeing her like that.

But then her lids fluttered opened, and she tried to smile weakly. "I knew you'd come. Always my rescuer."

Something in her voice made Grant frown. "The doctor says he's having a hard time keeping you calm. What's wrong?"

"I'm afraid I've got a deathbed confession to make." Her voice was weak, but Grant had little trouble understanding her.

His frown deepened. "Don't talk like that."

"Oh, don't worry. I'll pull through. I always do, don't I?"

"You're a fighter," he agreed.

She laughed softly. "If you only knew."

"What's that supposed to mean?"

She paused, gathering her strength. "Do you remember back in school when you used to have your friends over to play football in the backyard? I'd sit out on that little balcony off my room and watch you."

"You were my biggest fan," Grant said.

"Did you really think so?"

The sarcasm in her tone surprised him. "Vanessa, what's this all about?" he asked uneasily.

"Remember how you used to go on all those ski trips in the winter? And in the summer, how you and Grandfather went to his fishing cabin in Canada?"

"I remember," Grant said. "But I don't understand what your point is."

She paused again. "The point is, I never got to go. I never got to do any of the things you did."

Grant was helpless to know what to say. "I'm sorry."

She turned and met his gaze. Something glittered in her eyes. Something that was painful for Grant to see.

"Do you have any idea how much I resented you when we were growing up?" she asked.

He shook his head. "I never knew."

"Of course you did." Her smiled turned brittle. "You just didn't want to admit it."

Grant shrugged. "It doesn't matter now. That was a long time ago."

She drew a shallow breath. "Not as long ago as you think. The ski trips and the fishing and all that other stuff were bad enough, but what I really resented you for was the way Grandfather groomed you to take over Chambers Petroleum. He never even considered that the company was my heritage, too."

She rested for a moment, and Grant thought that she was finished. She'd unburdened her conscience, and now she could go back to sleep. But when he would have moved away from her bed, she caught his hand.

"You never knew this, but I went to Daddy once and told him how much I wanted to be a part of that company. I thought if anyone would understand, he would. I was always his favorite. But you know what he did? He brushed me off. He told me I didn't need to worry about Chambers Petroleum, because you and he would take care of it, just like you'd always taken care of me. I was twenty years old, and he treated me like a child. Worse than that. Like an invalid. That's the way you've always treated me, too, Grant."

He started to protest, but then stopped. Maybe she was right. Maybe he'd gone too far in trying to protect her. Maybe he should have let her stand on her own two feet a long time ago.

"After that, Chambers Petroleum became a symbol of everything I'd always wanted and couldn't have. Of everything that had always come so easy for you. I wanted there to be at least one thing you couldn't have. It only seemed fair. Just look at you…" She trailed off and lifted her hand, displaying the IV needle. "And look at me."

"Vanessa—"

"No, let me finish. I want to." She drew a labored breath, but when Grant would have protested again, she gave him a warning look. What else could he do but let her talk? It seemed to have a strange, calming effect her.

"One day when I came to the office, I met Clayton. Daddy had just hired him, and I knew the moment I laid eyes on him, he could give me what I wanted. All I had to do was get rid of you. And I did."

"What do you mean?

"I'm the one who hired your ex-girlfriend to claim her son was yours. I'm the one who created the scandal to discredit you in Daddy's eyes. And it worked better than I ever imagined. I couldn't believe it when he sent you to Venezuela for four years. That gave me plenty of time to marry Clayton and convince Daddy to make him vice president. And I knew if Clayton and I presented Daddy with his first grandson, the deal would be all but sealed.''

Grant stared at his sister, seeing a stranger. ''I can't believe what you're telling me.''

''Why? Because you didn't think I was capable of coming up with such a brilliant plan?'' Her tone was ironic.

He shook his head. ''I had no idea you were capable of such deception.''

''Well, now you do know,'' she said. ''And you haven't heard anything yet.''

Her words sent a chill of dread coursing through Grant. ''I'm almost afraid to ask what you mean.''

''Because you know what's coming, don't you?'' she asked softly, the first sign of regret showing in her eyes. She blinked and glanced away. ''The only hitch in my plan came when I found out I couldn't have children. Without an heir, Clayton didn't stand a chance to take over the company when you returned. You know how Daddy feels about family. About heirs.''

Grant's heart had begun to beat in painful strokes against his chest. ''What are you saying, Vanessa?''

She met his gaze almost defiantly. ''I'm saying John David isn't my son. He's *her* son.''

Dear God, Grant thought. *Nina had been right all along.* How blind he'd been not to see it.

''How could you do something like that, Vanessa? How could you take another woman's baby and pretend it was yours? How could you put her through that?''

"I just didn't let myself think about Nina at all. She was a means to an end, and everything would have been fine if she hadn't seen me in the park that day." Vanessa glanced at Grant accusingly. "In a way, this is all your fault, too. You were the one who convinced me to let Alice and John David spend the afternoon in the park, remember? After that, things just got out of control."

"You mean like Ruthanne Keller's death? The fire in Nina's office? My God, Vanessa, what have you done?" He stared at her, wondering how he could have missed the clues.

For the first time, fear sparked in her eyes. "I didn't kill that woman, and I didn't start the fire in Nina's house. I didn't set the fire at the hospital that night, either. I never wanted to hurt anyone. But now—"

She broke off, gasping for breath. The monitor beside her bed measured the acceleration of her heartbeat.

Grant jumped up in alarm. "Vanessa—"

She grabbed his hand. "Don't you see? It's all out of my control now. Nina's forced his hand, and now the only way out for him is to get rid of her."

"Who?" Grant asked urgently. "Who are you talking about?"

Vanessa's face had grown deathly pale. She clutched her chest. "Grant—"

His heart went into overdrive. "Just lie still. I'll go get help."

He jerked open the door to the hallway and called for the nurse, but Vanessa's monitor had already alerted the desk. A team of doctors and nurses rushed down the hall toward him.

They pushed Grant out of the way. "You'll have to leave now, sir," one of the nurses told him, shoving him toward the door. "We have to have room to work."

They crowded around Vanessa's bed until Grant could hardly see her. "Is she going to be all right?"

"Sir, please. You'll have to wait outside."

Grant allowed himself to be ushered into the hallway. He stood staring at Vanessa's door, watching the activity around her bed as an overwhelming sense of dread came over him.

It's all out of my control now. Nina's forced his hand, and now the only way out for him is to get rid of her.

Grant closed his eyes, feeling torn in two directions. His sister lay in that room, fighting for her life, while Nina was out there somewhere, alone and in danger.

He watched the frantic activity in Vanessa's room for a moment longer, knowing that she was receiving the best medical care possible. Knowing deep inside that he had always done everything he could for her.

Grant drew a long breath. There was nothing else he could do for his sister. But Nina, the woman he loved, was out there somewhere, and her life was in danger. Without hesitation, he turned and strode toward the elevators.

BY THE TIME Nina had gotten out of the shower and pulled on her nightgown and robe, she told herself she was feeling stronger. She could deal with Grant now, but the trouble was, he hadn't followed her home as she'd expected him to. He hadn't even called. Did that mean he'd heard the phone message from his father? Did he realize the jig was up?

Nina pulled her robe tighter as she paced her bedroom. First thing in the morning, she would consult an attorney. After everything that had happened, surely she could find a lawyer who would believe her. And if she couldn't, she'd find another way to take on the Chamberses and the Baldwins. She'd do whatever necessary to get her son back—

A noise inside the house startled Nina. She paused, listening. The sound came again, and her heart jumped to her throat. Someone was inside the house with her.

As quietly as she could, Nina moved to the bedroom door. Her first instinct was to lock it and then call the police before climbing out her bedroom window. But before she could close the door, a shadow moved in the hallway.

Nina gasped, and tried to slam the door, but the shadow flew down the hallway and a body rammed against the wood. Nina tumbled backward to the floor. The figure, all in black, was on her before she could move. Nina began to struggle, but the cold metal of a gun barrel against her temple stilled her.

"Good girl," said a voice she recognized.

"Trent," she whispered.

He whipped off the ski mask and smiled down at her. "Long time no see, Nina. Although I've been keeping close tabs on you. You just didn't know it."

Nina realized that all her fears had suddenly come true. Trent had come to get even with her for his brother's death.

"What do you want?" she asked with more force than she actually felt.

"I want you to shut up and stop making trouble for me."

"I don't know what you're talking about." Nina tried to shift from under him, but the gun barrel pressed more tightly against her head.

"I'm talking about John David, Nina. You can't keep claiming he's your son."

She looked at him in shock. "Why do you care?"

"Because if he turned out to be your son, that would mean he's my nephew, now wouldn't it? And I can't have that. I can't have you or your brat claiming any part of Garrett's trust fund. Thirty million dollars is a lot of money, Nina. Too much for the likes of you."

She struggled to keep up with him. "My brat?" she gasped. "Are you saying—?"

"That he's your son? Of course I am."

In spite of the situation, joy spiraled through Nina. John David was her son! He really was Dustin!

Trent must have seen the look of exultation on her face, for he said, "Don't get too excited about it, Nina. You're never going to see him again."

She ignored his threat. The revelation that John David was hers emboldened her. "You took him from the hospital, didn't you? It was you all along. How did you get Vanessa to go along with you?"

"It wasn't hard. I found out how desperate she was for a baby the day after you called me and told me you were pregnant. The plan just sort of evolved on its own."

"With Dr. Mapleton's help."

"Well, naturally. We had to have a professional.

He even took the pictures of Vanessa in front of the hospital with a prosthesis under her shirt. Everyone was convinced she was pregnant, and because she was confined to the hospital, even Clayton was never the wiser. Then you had to come along making trouble.''

Nina stared up at him. "How could you do it? Your own brother's baby."

"It's not like I sold him into slavery or anything. Hell, the kid's going to grow up in the lap of luxury."

"But to set a hospital on fire... My God, you could have killed innocent people."

Something flashed in Trent's eyes. Nina wanted to believe it was madness, but she knew better. He wasn't insane. He was just ruthless.

"The fire was just another happy coincidence," he said. "Vanessa, in her little Karen Smith disguise, was lurking in the hallway, pretending to be your sister until she saw a chance to snatch the baby. When the fire broke out, she simply took advantage of the situation." He stared down at her. "Now, the fire here. That's a different story."

"And Ruthanne Keller?"

"An unfortunate casualty. Couldn't have her recognizing Vanessa, now could I?"

Nina's heart pounded against her chest. She realized just how dangerous Trent really was, and how hopeless her situation seemed. There had to be a way out, she thought. There had to be. She had too much to live for to stop fighting now.

"What about the woman pretending to be Karen?"

He shrugged. "An actress. If Farrell digs deeply

enough, he'll find that out, but I don't expect he will. Not after tonight.''

"Tonight?" Nina asked, to keep him talking. She kept a flashlight under her bed for emergencies. If she could reach it, she would at least have a weapon, puny as it would be against Trent's gun.

"The investigation will be dropped after your suicide, Nina. The police, like everyone else, will be only too glad to have you out of their hair.''

Nina's hand closed over the cool metal of the flashlight. "But I don't even own a gun. They'll have to question that.''

"Not if you use Garrett's gun. You see, I really have thought of everything.''

"Not everything," Grant's voice said from the doorway.

In the split second Trent turned, Nina brought the flashlight up and smashed it against his temple. He fell back long enough for her to scramble away from him. In an instant, Grant was on him. The gun flew from Trent's hand, and both men lunged for it. Trent reached the weapon first and grabbed it, but before he could aim, Grant's hand closed around his wrist. The two men struggled for what seemed to Nina an eternity.

She lifted the flashlight again, but when she would have struck, the two men rolled over and Trent was suddenly on bottom. The gun was between the two men. Nina heard fists connect and grunts of pain before gunfire exploded and she screamed.

For the longest moment, no one moved. Then Grant toppled over. Nina's breath caught in her throat as she rushed toward him.

"Oh, God. Oh, dear God." His shirt was covered

in blood, but Nina saw almost immediately that he was alive. She sobbed in relief.

Grant sat up and took her in his arms. "I'm okay. It's all over." He glanced at Trent's prone body. "We'd better call an ambulance."

He got to his feet and helped Nina up, guiding her out of the bedroom. She stood at the window while he called 911, then he came to join her.

She turned to face him. "I found out tonight that John David is my son."

He nodded grimly. "I know. Vanessa told me earlier."

Nina looked at him in surprise. "She did?"

"I know everything."

Nina drew a long, ragged breath. "So do I. Your father called earlier and left a message on your machine. He said you were to find a way to get rid of me before Vanessa was released from the hospital. He made it sound as if you'd been planning against me all along."

"So that's why you left." Grant took her arm. "It wasn't like that. I'd told my father I would handle the situation. I thought I could find a way to end all this without anyone getting hurt." He winced, glancing at the bedroom. "All I ever wanted to do was help you find your son, Nina. I know that must be hard for you to believe right now."

The blood on the front of his shirt was a brutal reminder of how close she'd come to losing her life tonight. But Grant had saved her. Did anything else really matter?

"I do believe you," she said simply.

He took her in his arms as police sirens screamed in the distance.

Epilogue

A week had passed since the night Trent Fairchild had been killed. In the ensuing days, the truth about Nina's baby had come out. Vanessa had confessed everything to the police, and now it was only a matter of time and red tape before Nina's son would be returned to her. She'd learned the hard way that the wheels of justice sometimes turned slowly.

But I can be patient, she thought, standing in the yellow-and-white nursery. She'd waited all these months for Dustin to return home. She could wait a few days longer.

"But it had better not be too long," she muttered, placing a new teddy bear inside the crib. She touched the yellow plaid quilt longingly.

The doorbell sounded, and she reluctantly left the nursery to go answer the door. When she drew it back, her heart almost stopped.

Grant stood on the other side of the door, a suitcase at his feet and Dustin, dressed in a tiny baseball jacket and cap, in his arms.

Nina crossed her hands over her heart as she stared at them. How many times had she dreamed of such a moment?

"Aren't you going to ask us in?" Grant finally said.

She stepped back, still speechless. Tears stung her eyes, and her throat knotted painfully.

Grant turned the baby so he was facing her. "I don't believe you two have been formally introduced. Nina, this is your son. John—Dustin, this is Mommy."

Nina didn't know a heart could hold so much joy. She lifted her arms, and to her utter delight, her son reached for her. She took him and held him close, not ever wanting to let him go.

But Dustin would have none of that. He squirmed in her arms so that he could look up adoringly at Grant, who chucked him gently under the chin. "Do you know what a lucky kid you are?"

"I'm the lucky one," Nina whispered. "I can't believe this day has finally come."

Grant closed the door, and they walked inside together. Nina sat on the couch, turning the baby in her lap so she could stare down into his precious little face. Grant sat beside her, and for the longest moment, they said nothing while Dustin happily chewed a rattle Grant produced from his pocket.

"He's the most beautiful baby I've ever seen," Nina said finally.

"I would agree with that," Grant said. "He looks exactly like his mother."

Nina cocked her head, staring at the baby. "You really think so?"

"I don't know why I never noticed before," Grant said. "That must be why you seemed so familiar to me in the park."

Nina didn't want anything to cloud the joy of this day, but she had to ask, "How is Vanessa?"

Grant frowned, glancing away. "She has a long recovery ahead of her. My father has hired a team of lawyers, and they've already been meeting with the D.A. Considering her health and the family's pull, I don't think she'll spend any time in jail." He turned back to Nina, his gaze shadowed. "Can you live with that?"

"I'm only human," Nina said. "A part of me wants her to pay for what she did to my son and me, but then I look at you, and I don't want you hurt any more than you already have been. You've been wonderful to me, Grant."

He put an arm around her shoulders, drawing her and the baby close. "Clayton has accepted a job out of the country. I expect Vanessa will join him as soon as she's able to travel. I don't think she'll be coming back."

Nina bit her lip. "I'm sorry for what your family is going through right now."

"None of this is your fault." His arm tightened around her. "The one good thing to come of all this is us."

He leaned down to kiss her, but Dustin grunted and banged him with his rattle.

"Take it easy, slugger," Grant said. "I see I'm going to have to teach you about sharing. That is, if it's okay with your mother."

Nina looked up at him and smiled. "I want you to be a part of his life. He adores you, Grant, and he'll need you. I'm really just a stranger to him."

"He seems pretty at home to me."

It was true. Nina marveled at how content her son

seemed in her arms. She took that as a good omen of things to come.

"But he's still going to need you, too," she said.

"And what about you?" Grant asked in a low voice that sent a thrill of excitement through Nina.

She drew a breath. "I need you, too. I want you in my life."

"Good. Because I'm not going anywhere." Grant kissed her then, in spite of Dustin's protests. "You're just going to have to get used to it, kid."

But Dustin didn't have time to argue. He was rubbing his eyes and settling into his mother's lap for a nap.

"I could hold him like this forever," Nina whispered.

"He isn't going anywhere, either," Grant said. "Why don't you put him down?"

Reluctantly Nina carried the baby into the nursery. After he was settled, she tiptoed from the room, but she made sure the door was open, so that she could hear him the moment he awakened.

Grant was standing at the window. Nina walked up beside him, and he put an arm around her and kissed the top of her head. "You know, it *is* pretty amazing that we were able to find each other, considering the circumstances."

"I don't think it's amazing at all." She wrapped her arms around his neck and drew him to her. "Because some things are meant to be," she whispered against his lips.

Lost & Found

All new...and filled with the mystery and romance you love!

SOMEBODY'S BABY
by Amanda Stevens in November 1998

A FATHER FOR HER BABY
by B. J. Daniels in December 1998

A FATHER'S LOVE
by Carla Cassidy in January 1999

It all begins one night when three women go into labor in the same Galveston, Texas, hospital. Shortly after the babies are born, fire erupts, and though each child and mother make it to safety, there's more than just the mystery of birth to solve now....

Don't miss this *all new* LOST & FOUND trilogy!

Available at your favorite retail outlet.

HARLEQUIN®
Makes any time special ™

What do you want for Christmas?

A DADDY FOR CHRISTMAS

'Tis the season for wishes and dreams that come true. This November, follow three handsome but lonely Scrooges as they learn to believe in the magic of the season when they meet the *right* family, in *A Daddy for Christmas.*

MERRY CHRISTMAS, BABY
by Pamela Browning

THE NUTCRACKER PRINCE
by Rebecca Winters

THE BABY AND THE BODYGUARD
by Jule McBride

Available November 1998
wherever Harlequin and Silhouette books are sold.

HARLEQUIN®
Makes any time special ™

Silhouette®

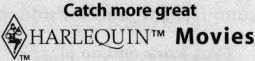 

MEN at WORK

All work and no play?
Not these men!

October 1998
SOUND OF SUMMER by Annette Broadrick

Secret agent Adam Conroy's seductive gaze could hypnotize a woman's heart. But it was Selena Stanford's body that needed saving—when she stumbled into the middle of an espionage ring and forced Adam out of hiding....

MEN IN UNIFORM

November 1998
GLASS HOUSES by Anne Stuart

Billionaire Michael Dubrovnik never lost a negotiation—until Laura de Kelsey Winston changed the boardroom rules. He might acquire her business...but a kiss would cost him his heart....

MILLIONAIRE'S CLUB

December 1998
FIT TO BE TIED by Joan Johnston

Matthew Benson had a way with words and women—but he refused to be tied down. Could Jennifer Smith get him to retract his scathing review of her art by trying another tactic: tying him *up?*

MAGNIFICENT MEN

Available at your favorite retail outlet!

MEN AT WORK™